Suddenl
was ov
staggering

Had he not been holding so tightly on to his splintered ego, he might have made an attempt to reach out to this shadowy vision of his past, envelop her in his arms and offer her a measure of comfort on this sad, dreary day.

Bewildered by the idea, he abruptly announced, "I've got to feed the stock. Make yourself at home."

"I'll do that," Melodie replied evenly, starting toward her old room, certain that nothing in this old house had changed at all.

But what she discovered behind that familiar closed door was enough to send her reeling.

Books by Cathleen Connors

Love Inspired

A Home of Her Own #167

CATHLEEN CONNORS,

a Wyoming native, teaches English to students in grades 6-12 in a rural school that houses kindergartners and seniors in the same building. She feels blessed to have married a man who is both supportive and patient. When she's not busy writing, teaching or chauffeuring her sons to and from various activities, she can most likely be found indulging in her favorite pastime—reading.

A Home of Her Own
Cathleen Connors

Love Inspired®

Published by Steeple Hill Books™

STEEPLE HILL BOOKS

Steeple
Hill™

ISBN 0-373-87174-0

A HOME OF HER OWN

Copyright © 2002 by Cathleen Galitz

Visit us at www.steeplehill.com

Printed in U.S.A.

Jabez prayed to the God of Israel:
"Oh, that you may truly bless me
And extend my boundaries
That your hand would be with me
And that you would keep me from evil."
And God granted his prayer.
—*1 Chronicles* 4:10

To Joan, whose unwavering faith
and gentle guidance have been a constant in the
Connors family for as long as I can remember.

Chapter One

The sound of snow crunching beneath Melodie Coleman's boots echoed in the empty caverns of her heart. Details that accompanied each step along the familiar pathway seemed to leap out at her. It felt so surreal that had she happened past a mirror she wouldn't have been much surprised to see herself as she looked at twelve years of age. A toothy tomboy clad in jeans, her twin blond braids slung carelessly over her shoulders. Eyes bright with hope. An irrepressible spirit as yet untouched by the perversity of fate.

Blinking against the spitting snow, she wondered how many snowmen she had erected in this same front yard only to see them dissolve into puddles over time.

Like her dreams.

Bending down as if to attend to one of the struggling flowers her mother insisted on planting along this pathway every spring, Melodie brushed at her eyes with the back of her hand. There were no blossoms, of course. It was snowing in the high country, and her mother would be planting no more seeds. Bulbs separated and nurtured by those gentle, hardworking hands lay as dormant beneath the frozen ground as Melodie's faith in herself. And in God, for that matter.

Melodie! Melodie Anne Fremont! You get in here this instant. Your dinner's getting cold.

Straightening at the sound of her mother's voice echoing in her memory, she could almost see Grace Fremont standing in the doorway waiting for her. Despite the scolding tone of her voice, there was a smile upon her weathered face as wide as the open expanse of the wilderness abutting their property.

Oh, how Melodie longed to drop the vestiges of time and run headlong into that blithe memory, to bury herself in her mother's forgiving arms and breathe deeply of the spices that always surrounded her. Instead she stood rooted to her spot, wishing only happy ghosts awaited her behind that closed door.

She forced herself to move forward. Each step was as leaden as her frame of mind. Fingering the key in her pocket, she halted on the front porch and contemplated the old brass knocker screwed into the front door. How strange it was to stand here wondering whether to knock or not. After all, the home in which she had been raised belonged to her now. Yet after so many years away, it felt presumptuous to barge right in.

What is the proper way to greet specters of the past?

I'm home, Mom, she wanted to call out. Like the prodigal son, she yearned to openly admit her mistakes and beg forgiveness. *You were right all along. Marrying Randall Coleman was the biggest mistake of my life. I'm sorry for hurting you. For disappointing you. So very sorry...*

Unlike the fortunate lad in the Bible, it was too late for Melodie to make amends. Too late to tell her mother how much she loved her. Too late to ask forgiveness for cutting off all but the most superficial of contact during her terrible bout with cancer. Too late for self-redemption.

Instead of the joyous reunion she had envisioned, Melodie was here to lay her mother to rest.

Snow on April Fools' Day seemed truly fitting. Fool that she was, the wide-eyed girl who had left home so long ago to find a destiny broader than the piece of land that was her heritage stood upon her own stoop a bona fide failure. Failing not only in her marriage but also in her obligation to her widowed mother. Taking the cold, smooth metal of the knocker into her hand, she rapped twice upon the door certain that nothing in her life could ever be harder than facing her mother's memory.

Nothing except being greeted by the man she jilted so long ago.

And had regretted losing every day since.

The door to her past swung open without so much as a creak.

"I've been expecting you," he drawled in a way that haunted Melodie's dreams to this day. "For quite some time."

The irony of his words was not lost on either of them.

"Hello, Buck," she said casually over the hammering of her heart. "You're looking good."

It was a gross understatement. Time had turned the gangly beau she remembered into as fine looking a man as could be found gracing the pages of any slick magazine ads. In truth, Buck Foster was far more appealing than any of those glistening boy toys with their fake smiles and steroid-enhanced muscles. His worn boots matched a pair of jeans that accentuated the fact that this was a real working cowboy. Melodie wondered if that Western-cut shirt he was wearing had been custom tailored to accommodate his well-muscled upper body. One good flex would surely rip the seams out.

You've filled out nicely, she almost blurted out. Not that such drop-dead good looks needed to be underscored by any such fawning observations.

Buck's broad shoulders filled the doorway, blocking her as effectively as any bouncer intent on keeping riffraff out of an establishment. Hair the color of dark, spiced rum showed no hint of gray yet. It was styled just as she remembered it in a no-nonsense manly cut that made Melodie smile inwardly. Needless to say, an upscale salon like the one Randall had frequented would hold no allure for a man such as Buck Foster.

She stuck her trembling hands into her pockets.

How did I ever let this one get away? she asked herself.

Stupidity. Sheer stupidity came the resounding response.

Memories, long suppressed, washed over her. It was with a certain amount of embarrassment that she remembered how hard she'd worked just to get him to notice her all those years ago. If Buck had any awareness of her girlish crush on him back then, he'd never so much as given a hint of it. Melodie recalled with aching tenderness the times she perched herself atop the corral fence like some raucous love bird, chattering inanely. It was upon that splintery old fence that she had fallen hopelessly in love with her mother's hired hand, the one that everyone in the community was so quick to condemn.

One day in particular stuck in her mind. It seemed it happened just yesterday. A wild-eyed bronco had just tossed Buck into the air like some rag doll, leaving him to take cover in the dust amid a flurry of hooves. Tears streaming down her face, Melodie screamed in alarm.

With all the dignity he could muster, Buck had picked himself up off the ground, dusted himself off and limped over to where she sat clenching the rail fence in white-knuckle terror. She'd urged her heart to start beating again as he braced himself by placing both hands on either side of her trembling body. It seemed that the entire world was contained in the span of Buck's loving arms. The scent of horseflesh and sweat and blood and pure cowboy filled her lungs. She feared she might actually swoon as he proceeded to brush aside her tears with the pad of his thumb.

"Don't you worry about me, Little Bit," he'd assured her. "I'm indestructible."

Vowing to be the one to prove him wrong, Melodie threw her arms around his neck and whispered fiercely, "No you're not. You're far more breakable than you know."

He'd laughed, and the sound had inflated her heart like a cheap red balloon.

"Thanks for your concern," he'd said. "Nobody else ever much cared whether I lived or died."

The memory alone still had the power to dust Melodie's flesh with goose bumps.

Seeing her shiver, Buck reluctantly stepped out of the way.

"Since you own the place," he growled, "I guess there's no need to invite you in."

Deliberately avoiding his eyes, Melodie trained hers on the middle button of his shirt—right where his heart used to be before she'd ripped it out and fed it to the wolves. It took every ounce of Buck's self-restraint to keep from slamming the door right in her face. A face, he noted with a trace of all too human satisfaction, that looked far more drawn than he remembered it.

In comparison to his six-foot-two-inch frame, Melodie looked very small indeed standing there upon the front step like some stranger stranded in a freak spring storm. Little Bit he used to call her when she was just a tagalong pest clamoring for his attention. Buck could discern no sign of that impish child in the tired-looking woman standing before him. Years of bitterness and anger left him unprepared for the sight of her looking so vulnerable and still so darned pretty with snowflakes clinging to those unbelievably long eyelashes.

Something twisted painfully in Buck's chest. He had once heard that amputees could actually feel an itch in their missing limbs. Maybe he was experiencing similar symptoms.

Hating himself for feeling anything at all for this woman, he donned a sardonic smile.

"Welcome home, Little Bit," he said, gesturing as grandly as any of the butlers he'd seen portrayed on television. He was not, however, moved to carry the charade so far as to help her off with her coat.

She shrugged it off without comment and hung it on the wooden peg in the entryway. Though made of wool, the garment was inadequate for Wyoming's harsh weather—much like its owner, Buck thought ruefully to himself. Its classic Southwestern design was slightly out of place as well, serving as a reminder that this native had abandoned her birthplace for the warmer clime of Arizona.

Melodie flinched at the sound of the old endearment that Buck flung so carelessly at her feet. She had forgotten how cold this little house could get, and the chilly reception she'd received nudged the temperature several degrees lower. Memories of her mother standing at the stove came back to her with all the pungency of Grace's mouthwatering cinnamon apple pie. So strong was the image that Melodie almost stepped up to the stove to warm her cold derriere like she had in times gone by.

Unfortunately without her mother's love to warm it, the little house was as frosty and unwelcoming as Buck's eyes. Those amber orbs reminded her of a cougar warily sizing up its prey.

Focusing on her surroundings seemed safer than meeting those eyes directly. The faded floral wallpaper in the kitchen seemed as depressing to Melodie as the matching mail-order curtains that hung limply over the sink. Linoleum, scratched and freckled by the sun, was beginning to curl in the corners. Dusty knickknacks seemed glued to their spots on equally dusty shelves. Nothing much seemed to have changed since Melodie's childhood—other than the fact that everything seemed smaller, colder, paler....

Like a corpse set out for viewing.

Melodie shuddered at the thought of tomorrow's funeral. Sagging wearily into a pearl-colored vinyl chair, she rested her elbows on the matching dinette table and allowed herself a heartfelt sigh.

"Sorry to hear about Randall," Buck offered, his voice flat.

Guarded.

Melodie glanced at him sideways trying to discern just how much he knew about her husband's death. She so hoped to leave that heartache behind her in the deserts of Arizona. The last thing she needed right now was to be reminded that she was supposed to be a grieving widow when, in fact, it was her mother's passing that truly left her feeling gutted and bereft. As tragic as Randall's suicide several weeks ago had been, it had given Melodie a sense of freedom denied her throughout their complicated and troubled marriage. As it was impossible to gauge Buck's sincerity, she merely nodded her head to acknowledge his proffered condolences. Genuine or not, she appreciated his civility under such strained circumstances.

"Would it be too much to ask for a cup of coffee?" she asked, deliberately changing the subject.

At the request, Buck's expression tightened. He'd be hanged if he was going to wait on her. He wasn't the same whipped, eager to please, little puppy she remembered anticipating her every whim.

"Do I look as if I have Maitre d' stamped on my forehead?"

A smile twitched at one corner of Melodie's mouth. "Not that I can see," she admitted. Gesturing toward the coffeepot on the counter, she asked, "Mind if I help myself?"

"Knock yourself out."

Accepting his open hostility with the tiniest of shrugs, she rose to her feet and crossed to the cupboards. It came as no surprise to find the cups exactly where she remembered them, lined up behind the jelly jars that served as juice glasses. Melodie felt a twinge of irritation. Where was the expensive set she'd sent her mother? Probably gathering dust in the back of a closet with the rest of her gifts or possibly rewrapped and recycled as a present for someone "more needy."

Melodie picked up the mug closest to her. The words To Mother With Love were handpainted across the dull white enamel and emblazoned with foolish-looking tulips. It had been Grace's favorite, a Mother's Day gift from her second-grade daughter. The rim was chipped, the handle had been glued back on and much of the paint had not survived countless washings.

It seemed that her mother's entire life was embodied in that sentimental mug. A life spent in selfless devotion to others. A life based on the principles of hard work and an unwavering faith in God. A life so filled with frugality that no two glasses on the shelf matched.

Accepting for a fact that she in no way deserved the love that her mother had lavished on her since the day she'd been born, Melodie pulled the garbage can out from its concealed space beneath the sink and dropped the mug in. One by one she tossed in every single jelly glass as well. It was doubtful that Buck would have attempted to extract them as Grace surely would have done, but Melodie was nonetheless determined that every glass shattered as it hit its mark. The sound covered a muffled sob. Her tears glistened amid shards of broken glass.

Seeing her shoulders shake, Buck conjectured the cause of Melodie's distress. Once upon a time a mismatched table service would have held no shame for the sweet, guileless girl who had been raised within these four walls.

"Must be hard coming back here after living in a mansion," he ventured.

The tone behind that simple observation was

sharper than the icicle dagger he seemed intent upon driving through her back.

Fearing she might choke on them, Melodie chose her words carefully. "It's not that. It's just that she deserved better."

"Yes, she did," Buck agreed, biting back the oath scalding his tongue. "She deserved a whole lot better than what you gave her, and I'm not talking about a blasted set of dishes either!"

That cruel accusation caused Melodie to spin around on her heels. Eyes the color of a stinging winter sky snapped with indignation.

"And just what gives you the right to judge me? To sit as both judge and jury on my feelings for my mother?" she demanded.

Matching hers in intensity, Buck's eyes threatened to burn a hole right through her.

"Years of being by her side, watching her scrimp and save to leave you a 'respectable' inheritance, months of holding her hand and watching her waste away from cancer and heartache as she waited for any scrap of attention you might deem to send long-distance."

"Self-righteous words from the dutiful son my mother never had. Between her sainthood and your martyrdom, I doubt if there would have been

enough room at her bedside for a sinner like me!''
Melodie snarled in return.

Despite the vehemence of her response, Melodie's shoulders slumped beneath the weight of her
guilt. Sucker punched by Buck's resentment, she
turned aside to hide the depth of her pain. Placing
both hands on the dated Formica countertop, she
attempted to steady herself. Her hands were still
trembling when she reached for the coffeepot and
poured herself a cup. As if hoping to somehow
warm herself all the way through with its meager
heat, she wrapped her fingers tightly around it before turning back around to face her grand inquisitor.

What possible good would come from trying to
explain that Randall wouldn't *let* her come home?
That juggling a demanding job and a manic-depressive husband simultaneously was all she had
been able to manage at the time. The excuse
sounded pathetic even to her own ears. Squaring
her slender shoulders, Melodie strode back to the
table with her chin tilted defiantly up. Taking her
seat, she brought the cup to her lips to blow away
the steam that rose like an incantation from the
dark brew.

The silence was deafening. They looked at one
another more as strangers separated by strands of

barbed wire than as one-time soul mates. Swishing a sip of hot liquid around in her mouth, Melodie forced herself to swallow it along with yet another tough piece of leftover pride.

"Look, Buck," she began, daring to meet his eyes dead on. "You're certainly entitled to your feelings, and God knows I owe you a debt of gratitude not to mention a long overdue apology. But it's unlikely that the years of hurt between us are going to be healed over any cup of coffee. Since we've both got a couple of hard days ahead of us, do you think we could postpone our mutual animosity until after the funeral?"

For the first time since she had stepped inside the house, his features visibly softened.

Taking in the hard line of Melodie's jaw and the way her throat pulsed as it closed around unshed tears, Buck realized just how near she was to breaking down. After years of cherishing the idea, he was surprised to discover how distasteful the actual possibility was.

Unbidden memories tugged at his conscience as he recalled the last conversation he'd had with her mother.

Don't be too hard on my little girl when she comes home, Grace had begged him on her deathbed. *She was awful young when she hurt you, and you don't know what kind of struggles she's had to endure these past years.*

Buck didn't dare squeeze the frail hand that clutched his. Grace's bones were brittle, her skin almost translucent, her eyes dark hollows of concern—ever filled with concern for the daughter who had abandoned them both.

I won't, he had replied over the bile that rose in his throat.

There was little Buck could refuse Grace. Abandoned as a child by an alcoholic single mother with the morals of an alley cat, he spent years being bounced from foster family to foster family. Grace had literally snatched him off the road to the reform school when she offered him a job.

And a home.

And an opportunity to be accepted for who he was and what he had to contribute to their family. She had treated him as if he truly were her flesh and blood. Although she pleaded with her eyes, Grace had not openly asked him to forgive her daughter. Buck was grateful for that. Some things were simply too reprehensible to warrant forgiveness, and being cheated on was one of them. He wasn't likely to ever forget the fact that Melodie had made a fool of him. A broken heart is hard enough to heal in private, but when a proud man is made the target of public snickering, it is often easier to simply discard his heart than to attempt resuscitating something damaged beyond repair.

While Melodie waited for a response to her request for a temporary truce, she stiffened her nerves with another shot of caffeine. She could almost feel the strong, black coffee eating away the lining of her empty stomach.

"Fair enough," Buck conceded grudgingly. "I suppose the least either of us could do for Grace is call a cease-fire for the time being."

"Thank you," she said, rising on shaky legs. "I guess I'd better get started unpacking."

Buck did not respond with so much as a grunt let alone an offer to help her bring in her luggage. Facing his past had proven harder than he'd imagined. In recurring dreams, he'd told this woman exactly what he thought of her, lashing out with brutal honesty until she melted into a puddle of remorse at his feet. Oddly enough, now that the moment had come, he found he simply didn't have the heart for it. Grace had always maintained that vengeance should be left to the Lord. Maybe she was right. Looking into Melodie's guarded eyes, Buck saw a glimpse of someone who'd been through hell on earth. He doubted whether anything he had to say would penetrate the protective mask she was wearing. That brittle facade was so firmly fixed in place that he wondered if behind it there remained a single trace of the sweet girl with whom he had once upon a time fallen so desperately in love.

Suddenly his anger was overcome by a staggering sense of loss. What was the use of venting so many years after the fact? What could possibly be gained by inflicting even more pain upon one another now? Having embraced Grace's faith some time ago, he recalled God's admonition to forgive others as we would have others pardon our transgressions. Had he not been holding so tightly on to his splintered ego, Buck might have made an attempt to reach out to this shadowy vision of his past, envelop her in his arms and offer her a measure of comfort on this sad, dreary day.

Bewildered by the very idea, he abruptly announced, "I've got to feed the stock. Make yourself at home."

Melodie glanced at him sharply. Was the remark intended to be as caustic as it had sounded? Surely he wasn't worried that she was going to throw him out of the only home he'd ever known? Or herself for that matter. While it was true that she had lived in finer places since she'd moved away, none had ever earned the privilege of feeling like a real home.

''I'll do that,'' she replied evenly, starting toward her old room with the same confidence with which she had approached the cupboards earlier, certain that nothing in this old house had changed at all.

But what she discovered behind that familiar closed door was enough to send her reeling.

Chapter Two

"I suppose you expected me to stay in the bunk-house forever?"

Melodie snapped her jaw back into place before attempting to address the question. The way Buck was leaning up against the wall prejudging her was so patently insolent that she didn't dare give him an honest reaction. She didn't think she could endure much more of his scoffing.

"Of course not," she lied.

It was, after all, a perfectly logical arrangement. Melodie simply couldn't bring herself to accept the fact that her mother had actually moved Buck into *her* old room. So secure had she been in the belief that this little house was impervious to change that it unnerved her to realize all vestiges of her presence had been completely erased from the room that had at one time been the center of her universe.

She had opened the door expecting to see everything in its place: her old stuffed animals, a prized collection of ceramic horses, a beloved Western doll with a leather fringed skirt and vest, her trophies lined up on the shelf along one wall, a coveted rodeo queen sash draped over the headboard of her twin bed, the embroidered quilt her mother had stitched with equal amounts of love and patience one Christmas when money was particularly scarce—all the special things that marked the passage of her youth.

Instead Melodie was met by stark walls devoid of anything more personal than a trophy fish mounted above Buck's four-poster bed. The room was tidy enough, she'd give him that. As neat as an orphan's scrapbook. She suspected that her mother was responsible for the only personal touch in the room: a handmade afghan folded neatly on the foot of a bed that quite simply overwhelmed the small area.

"Just tell me when you want me to move out."

Startled by the straightforwardness of Buck's

overture, Melodie hastened to reassure him that she
had no intention of uprooting him.

"N-never," she stammered over the tripping of
a heart too easily moved to sentimental palpita-
tions. "I'll just put my things in Mom's room."

Despite the glibness of her response, Buck's occupancy in her old room did present Melodie with
a new and unfathomable set of problems. She
couldn't imagine sleeping in the very next room to
the man whose heart she had accidentally broken
without ever fully explaining herself. A man who
had every right to hate her guts. A man whose
presence still had the power to make her very soul
tremble.

For one thing, the walls were paper-thin! she
thought to herself.

People were bound to talk, Buck thought to himself.

Indeed, gossip traveled faster than a brush fire
in this small community where everything was ev-
erybody's business. Pushing himself away from the
wall, Buck came to stand within inches of Melodie.
So close that he could smell her uniquely feminine
scent. That haunting blend of leather and lace,
sagebrush and musk, stirred memories of a time
when the world was as new to them as to a colt
surveying life for the first time on wobbly legs.

"Aren't you worried about your reputation, Little Bit?" he queried, cocking an eyebrow at her.

Her reputation! Melodie almost laughed out loud. If he only knew how little that tattered rag mattered to her.

"You were always a lot more worried about that than I was." Hearing the trace of bitterness in her voice, she hastened to add, "Besides I'm well past worrying what anyone else thinks, Buck."

Even you, she silently added.

Once upon a time she had allowed concern for fickle virtue to throw away a life with the gentle man who refused to bed her for the manipulative opportunist who had. What she had endured throughout the travesty of her marriage left Melodie numb to the threat of public ridicule.

She risked a small smile. "What about you? Are you worried about a wicked widow besmirching your honor?"

Buck snorted his derision at the idea.

"Once you've been dragged through the mud down the streets of this one-horse town, you get used to it."

Falling into his amber-colored eyes was like diving to the bottom of a glass of expensive bourbon, aged with pain. Melodie yearned to reach out and caress his rough cheek with an equally work-roughened hand, to smooth away his sorrows with a well-chosen, heartfelt apology.

I am so sorry, she longed to say, knowing she was the one responsible for his humiliation.

But sorry was such a useless word. It could neither bring back her mother, nor Randall, nor change the course of a life shaped by one horrible mistake.

Melodie opened her mouth to respond, but no words came out.

Buck left her standing there feeling rather like a guppy. The front door closed behind him with a sigh of regret. As if afraid of disturbing a single dust mote, she trod softly across what was now Buck's room. Melodie took a deep breath before entering. Assailed by the trace fragrance of lilacs that had been Grace's signature scent, she was instantly taken back to a vision of her mother as a young woman. Eyes the same vivid blue as her daughter's twinkled in a face as yet unlined by time.

"Oh, Mama," she whispered crossing the room in a few short steps. Sinking into the old brass bed, she felt her mother's ghost stir. Underlying the sweet, reminiscent essence of lilacs was the residual smell of medicine. And the lingering odor of death.

How could she possibly stay in this room?

Looking around, she found it more a shrine than a bedroom. The walls were covered with pictures of Melodie at all ages, each precocious stage immortalized on film. The only photograph in the room that did not prominently feature Melodie was Grace's wedding picture. From the bedstand, the father Melodie could not remember was blissfully unaware of his impending death. Tromped beneath a rodeo bull's hooves, this stranger had left his young wife and three-year-old daughter a rugged patch of land and little else.

Melodie was struck anew with awe for her mother's fortitude. A single woman raising a child and managing a ranch by herself had been unheard of at the time. An unlikely feminist, Grace Fremont had instilled in her daughter a sense of self-reliance that Melodie prayed would see her through yet another difficult time.

Grace's remedy for just about any given situation was a homemade concoction she'd perfected. The primary ingredients were tenacity, hard work and faith in God. In the end it hadn't been enough.

Melodie winced. It grieved her to think of her mother dying on the same bed in which she'd given birth to her only child. An ungrateful brat the world denounced for abandoning her in her time of greatest need. It pained her to think of her mother struggling from the beginning to the end of her hard-fought existence with little more comfort than could be derived from her well-worn Bible. The school of hard knocks had taught Melodie that one might as well wish upon a star as put her faith in a God who allowed good people to suffer so horribly with emotional and physical cancers.

Not that she had any special bragging rights to a better life herself, coming home as she did without a job, a husband, or a child to call her own. Coming home without so much as a heart beating inside her hollow chest. At twenty-five, Melodie's natural beauty, exuberance and religious beliefs had been tested daily by the elements and a loveless marriage that had left her feeling both undesirable and lacking.

Her eyes scanned the photographs lining the walls for happier memories. Her favorite was the one in which she wore a frilly prom dress looking far too much like a Southern belle to suit her tastes. The smile she wore was broad and genuine and filled with expectations of wondrous things to come. It was hard to remember a time when her smile wasn't tight and forced.

She almost didn't recognize the fresh-faced young man beaming beside her in his rented tuxedo. Gangly at twenty, Buck had not yet grown into his features. The look of unguarded affection etched upon that youthful face was so poignant that it caused a tiny whimper of pain to escape from some place deep inside Melodie.

She grabbed a pillow from the bed and hugged it tightly, willing herself not to cry. Stiff from the long drive, weary bones protested against being curled into a fetal ball. Her shoulders bunched into twin knots of tension.

How could she have been so careless with such a precious gift of love? Like forgotten friends gathered together for an unexpected reunion, memories crowded into the small room. A smile tugged at Melodie's heart as she recalled that long-ago prom.

It had taken some doing to convince Buck to go as her date. To him she had always been Little Bit, his employer's pesky kid. When she first approached him about the prom, Buck frankly told her that he hadn't much interest in going to such fancy doings when he had been in high school himself. In his early twenties, such a silly rite of passage held even less appeal for him.

But when Melodie confided red-faced that no one had asked her, his resistance softened. An outsider all of his life, Buck could certainly understand how she wouldn't want to go stag to her senior prom. He also knew that it would break her mother's heart not to see her only daughter all gussied up in that frothy pink formal she had been secretly sewing for the last month.

Buck would have just as soon cut off a hand as to see Grace Fremont hurt.

In truth, Melodie had known that Buck agreed to go to the prom with her more out of concern for her mother than for her. She never bothered telling him that she had, in fact, turned down two other young men who had sought her for their prom dates. Everything changed between them, however, when she came out of her room wearing a dress that showed off her budding curves, her flaxen hair swept up in a fashion that made her look older than her sixteen years. She watched a change come over Buck.

Little Bit was no more. In her place had stood a young woman who had every intention of making this man fall in love with her.

''Your boutonniere is outside,'' she'd told him shyly after he'd pinned a corsage to her dress. She hoped he wouldn't be embarrassed by such a simple token of her affection.

After Grace had taken her quota of photographs, Melodie had drawn Buck out of the house and into her mother's garden. While she selected a perfect white rosebud from her mother's prized blooms, she made him stand beneath the trellised archway that she hoped would someday be the focal point of their wedding. Beneath a rising moon and surrounded by the fragrant blossoms of a late spring, Melodie pinned the boutonniere to Buck's lapel. So strong and broad and appealing was his chest that she could not resist running her hands across its width.

"Kiss me," she had implored in a whisper so soft she wasn't sure he'd even heard it.

His arms reached around her lithe, young body and drew her near. Slowly he'd lowered his mouth to hers to brush her lips with a tender kiss.

Brushing blond tendrils from her glowing face, Buck had admitted his own vulnerability. "If you ever hope to get to that prom, we'd better get going. I'd hate to do anything to betray your mother's trust."

The knowledge that Melodie could exercise womanly powers over a creature so much bigger and stronger than she was heady stuff indeed.

Feeling like a real-life Cinderella, she claimed all of Buck's dances that magical evening as both reveled in the knowledge that before the sun set on the next day, everyone in town would know that they were a serious couple.

Nothing could have made Grace happier.

That summer after Melodie graduated and turned eighteen was truly enchanted. That was the summer they frolicked like colts and took every opportunity to steal kisses under a warm and gentle sun. That was the summer Melodie was crowned rodeo queen in the proud tradition of her mother and her grandmother before her. That was the summer Buck made up his mind to propose—but not before he could offer Melodie a lifestyle he felt she deserved. He put every dime he earned towards a ring at the local jeweler's and simultaneously made plans to build her a dream home with his own capable hands.

Buck had restrained his masculine desires, respecting the tenets of the religion Grace had worked so hard to instill in them both and vowing to wait until he could legally make her his bride.

Melodie punched the pillow she was holding and, in the fading light of her mother's bedroom, considered the aged water stains on the ceiling. How frustrated she had been that summer! In her mind she was all but throwing herself at Buck. Not coquettish by nature, she had employed every feminine wile in her limited power to let him know how desperately she wanted him. To no avail.

Rolling onto her stomach, Melodie rebuked herself for indulging in such sweet torture. Clinging to such tender memories all the while shaking her fist at the universe and reminiscing over what should have been served no useful purpose. No amount of wishful thinking was going to change history. She was here to make her amends with the past, to accept her responsibility in shaping it and to face the new day as her mother always had—bravely.

Dawn poked its rosy fingers through yellowed lace curtains and gently awakened Melodie to a new day. Eyes sticky with sleep, she was at first disoriented by her surroundings. It took a moment for her to discern that she had fallen asleep fully dressed upon her mother's bed and that somebody had thoughtfully covered her with a blanket. Undoubtedly the same somebody who had brought her luggage in from her vehicle and deposited them at the foot of the bed.

How curious it was to wake up to the smell of bacon and eggs! And how odd that it made her feel suddenly queasy. During the course of her married life, if Melodie failed to rise to the challenge of such simple chores, she simply went without eating. Randall had been hard-pressed to prepare anything more complicated than a bowl of cold cereal for himself. Melodie felt a twinge of guilt at the uncharitable thought. The poor man was dead. That she felt more relief than remorse at his passing was surely sinful in itself.

As if merely wishing for release from the bonds of his possessive love had somehow been the cause of his death.

Rubbing her eyes in hopes of erasing such irrational thoughts, Melodie dragged herself out of bed, ran a brush halfheartedly through her hair and decided that her rumpled state would simply have to do. She hadn't come home to compete in a beauty pageant. Besides, she'd wager Buck wouldn't give her a second glance if she walked into the kitchen wearing a diamond tiara. If ever there had been any doubt in her mind that he might still be yearning for her after all this time, his reaction to her yesterday set the record straight once and for all.

The old house wasn't pretentious enough to boast a dining room. Melodie opened the door of her mother's bedroom and walked the short distance to the kitchen where Buck greeted her with a civil, "Good morning."

She responded in kind, minus the *good*.

My, how that man could fill a room with his mere presence. Instinctively her hand went to her hair, making Melodie feel six shades a fool for even caring what he thought of how she looked.

"Did you sleep well?" he asked, handing her a plateful of steaming food.

Crooking an eyebrow at the polite inquiry, Melodie studied her scrambled eggs for any trace of arsenic.

"Fine," she answered sliding into her place at the table. "Thank you for breakfast. And for bringing in my luggage. You didn't have to do that. I was planning on getting to it first thing this morning."

Buck made an attempt at a smile. "I decided that you're right about putting our differences aside until after the funeral. After all, today's bound to be hard on you."

"And on you," Melodie allowed over the ball of emotion clogging her throat. "You know, I would understand if you want to take your own vehicle to the funeral rather than going with me."

The way he dismissed the suggestion with a wave of his hand was nothing short of mesmerizing. He'd always had such marvelous hands. Unlike Randall's manicured hands that had been fit more for a pencil than a pair of reins, Buck's hands were big and strong and marked by honest labor.

"That won't be necessary," he assured her.

"We're both grown-ups. Your mother would expect no less of us than to put aside old grudges today, so if you don't mind, I'll drive us both to the church."

Melodie could do no more than nod her head gratefully. It was too much to hope that his offer was motivated as much out of concern for her as out of respect for her mother. Separated only by the expanse of a scarred, old table, it was hard not to ponder how different her life would have been had she married Buck like her heart had instructed her instead of Randall as dictated by her conscience. A conscience shaped by the rigid dogma of a religion that had somehow convinced her that eternal occupancy in hell could be purchased by one youthful mistake. Had she but been able to turn her back on that conviction, Melodie wondered if all her days might have started out with coffee and conversation instead of her usual dosage of censure and silence.

Uncomfortable with the faraway look in Melodie's eyes, Buck bolted down his breakfast and hastened to leave, stating that he had to look after the livestock. Melodie envied him. She longed to take comfort in the kind of hard physical labor that had characterized her life. Buck wouldn't hear of it as he bade her get ready for the long day ahead.

After lingering over a breakfast left mostly untouched, Melodie considered the black suit that she intended to wear for this sad occasion. She had purchased it a short time ago and worn it only once—at her husband's funeral.

Slipping into the cool, black silk, Melodie relived that terrible day. Since her own mother had been too ill to travel the long distance to be at her side, she suffered through the ceremony alone. A few of Randall's engineering associates had shown up to pay their respect as well as some of the hired hands from the dude ranch that she had been managing. The modest gathering meant a great deal to Randall's parents who were so bereft at the loss of their only child that they could barely acknowledge his widow, a woman they had felt all along was beneath their son. They felt little need to offer Melodie any more than their condolences.

On some subconscious level, she felt herself entitled to little more. Beneath her black veil, Melodie was secretly relieved that the hand of fate rather than a legal document had dissolved her marriage. Not only was she convinced that Randall would have fought with all his might against a divorce, Melodie herself had been raised that once you make your bed, you sleep in it—crumbs and all. So she did her best to graciously accept the sympathy offered her without shattering anyone's image of a marriage that had always looked better from the outside than the inside.

Their duty done, Randall's friends scurried self-righteously back to their fancy Tucson offices to embrace the little calculators that ruled their world. Her in-laws returned to Denver to pick up the silken thread of their social lives, and Melodie proceeded to tender her resignation before the end of the week. Although far from feminine or traditional, her job was something she enjoyed and was good at. It also helped pay for all those expensive toys that Randall accumulated in a futile effort to look richer than he really was.

Melodie's boss, Peter Hamlein, hated to see her go. Initially he hadn't thought a woman capable of acting as head wrangler, but he'd been in a bind and decided to give her a chance. Melodie had proven him wrong, working long hours beside the men beneath the blistering Arizona sun and treating every aspect of the operation as if it were her own. Peter assured her that the work ethic she brought with her from Wyoming was in short supply in this snowbirds' paradise. In addition to her excellent horsewoman skills, Melodie was the best people person he'd ever had in the position. An important part of the job required placating the rich dudes who spent a fortune to be waited on hand and foot for the entirety of their vacations. Pete offered her more money in hopes of getting her to stay on, but she was clearly anxious to get home to her ailing mother. Melodie could offer him no more than a couple of weeks' notice to help him get things in order for her replacement.

She had been in the process of packing her bags when she received news of her mother's death.

Certain she couldn't make it through another funeral as bleak as Randall's, Melodie took comfort in the fact that many old friends and neighbors were sure to be in attendance today. Grace had been well liked and respected in the community as one of their most stalwart pioneers. Forcing her feet into a pair of dark pumps, Melodie walked over to her mother's cloudy mirror and surveyed her appearance. The dead look in her eyes came as no surprise. She pulled her long blond hair into a severe bun, pinned it down with forceful jabs, and waited for Buck to tell her it was time to go.

Chapter Three

Buck looked handsome in a Western-cut black suit that emphasized his lean muscularity and made him look rather like the CEO of an up-and-coming company on the verge of a hostile takeover. Ever the gentleman, he opened the passenger door of his pickup for Melodie and helped her in.

Feeling suddenly awkward in anything other than a comfortable pair of cowboy boots, Melodie struggled to gain her seat without revealing any more of her legs than necessary to the man, who even in this moment of deep apprehension, made her so totally aware of her long-forgotten womanly allure. Tensing beneath the tawny scrutiny of his eyes, she still felt his helping touch. Had he noticed how bow-legged she had become from living in a saddle?

Buck wasn't aware of any such imperfections as he allowed his gaze to trace the lines of the slender legs in question. Despite her efforts to make herself look plain, Melodie was as pretty and fragile as a china doll. Unadorned with anything other than naturally long lashes, her eyes appeared so large and luminous that a man could fall into their vulnerable depths and never find his way out. A sudden longing to free a single blond tendril from the captivity of that tight bun startled Buck. For the briefest fraction of a second, he considered reaching out to take the hands folded so demurely in Melodie's lap and offering her the solace of human touch on this sad day.

The thin gold band she still wore on her finger was an effective deterrent to that foolish impulse.

It rankled him to see her still wearing that ring.

Over the years Buck had come to conclude that the only thing that milksop Randall had over him was money and breeding. The money part didn't bother him much, but he was mighty sensitive about the fact that his mother had abandoned him as easily as she might have dumped a stray off at a shelter.

Thinking Melodie had jilted him for status and

money, over the years Buck had taken perverse comfort in casting her motives in a bad light. That she continued to wear her dead husband's ring indicated that she might have actually loved him. He wondered if that disagreeable taste in his mouth wasn't the lingering extract of jealousy.

Grace hadn't expounded about her son-in-law's untimely death when she informed him that Melodie was quitting her job managing that fancy dude ranch and finally coming home. They'd had a long, unspoken agreement never to mention Randall's name in each other's presence, and Grace wasn't one to break it—even if the fellow in question was dead. Buck was left, however, with the definite impression that Grace would not grieve his passing one iota more than he himself did.

A thin drizzle of rain spit against the windshield as Buck drove the short distance to the church where Grace had spent every Sunday morning since he had known her. And where he had accompanied her for the better part of the last two years. To his surprise, he found more peace within that humble little church than he had in all the years of trying to prove himself to a world he once thought completely against him. Framed against the backdrop of the majestic Pinnacle Mountains, the white chapel took on the modesty and serenity of a nun.

Though Buck would have preferred mingling Grace's ashes with the loam of her beloved mountains rather than boxing her into a formal ceremony constrained by four walls, he knew that the community needed the chance to publicly mourn the passing of one of their most faithful members.

He intentionally arrived early so that both he and Melodie could say their private farewells to the woman who meant so much to each of them.

Once inside, Melodie drew a sharp breath at the sight of the coffin positioned at the front of the church where she had been both baptized and confirmed. Inexplicably exhausted by the miles she had traveled, she had been in no shape to stop by the funeral home to pay her respects yesterday.

Buck squeezed her shoulder in sympathy. "You okay?"

Eyes wide with pain bespoke Melodie's trepidation at the task before her. Though Buck's presence beside her was reassuring, she nonetheless flinched at his touch. How could he be so kind to her in light of the way she had treated him?

The flash of hurt in his chiseled features indicated that her aversion to his touch did not go unnoticed.

"I'll give you a moment alone," he murmured, turning away before she could stop him.

For the sake of her sanity, Melodie concentrated on details of her surroundings as his footsteps faded away. Gathering clouds outside let little light through the stained-glass windows, lending gloominess to an already dismal day. She noticed that a soft green Berber had replaced the ugly gold shag carpet she remembered so well. Compelling herself up the center aisle one step at a time, she stood at last before the open coffin.

A suffocating sense of déjà vu grabbed her by the throat. Other than the fact that Randall's casket had been closed because of the manner in which he'd chosen to die, the scene itself was horribly familiar. Peering timidly over the side of the casket, Melodie struggled to keep from screaming, *What have you done with my mother?*

The withered body lying before her bore little resemblance to the vibrant woman Melodie remembered. She reached out to touch those loving hands folded so peacefully as if in prayer. And instantly recoiled from the icy contact with death.

How sad it was that she had nothing to give this woman who had given so much of herself. Not even her tears. Years of stoically keeping her feelings to herself had dried up any public display of emotion. Had she any faith left in God, Melodie could have offered her mother a prayer, but she knew only too well there was nothing she could do now to make up for the pain she had caused this dear woman.

No amount of pleading over a dead body would buy her the forgiveness Melodie was seeking.

Staring at her mother's age-blemished hands, it occurred to her that she did have a token to offer Grace after all. Years ago, her mother had expressed the desire to be buried with her wedding ring. Even in this small request it seemed circumstances had conspired against her. Ultimately the ring had been pawned to pay bills. With a sudden ferocity of intent, Melodie wrenched the gold band from her own finger and slipped beneath the hollow of her mother's folded hands the only thing of value Randall had left her.

"Rest in peace, Mamma," she whispered. "Nobody deserves it more than you."

The ceremony was brief and poignant, the small church filled to overflowing. A carry-in sponsored by the local church ladies followed in the basement that was as dark and drafty as Melodie remembered. Apparently recent attempts to raise money for a new parish hall had been met with complaints about the economy and flagging cattle prices. The good news was they had enough money in the fund last fall to do the groundwork and pour the foundation. Concerned members left the rest in God's hands. The condition of her surroundings mattered little to Melodie who was anxious to express her appreciation to those present for taking the time to pay their respects. Despite the sad circumstances of her homecoming, it was good to be back in the tight-knit community where she had been raised, and she was looking forward to reestablishing ties with old neighbors and friends.

Extending a hand to the woman who had been her mother's closest neighbor—a mere three miles down the lane—Melodie tried to keep her emotions in check. "It was very kind of you to come, Mrs. Linn."

As if fearing she would somehow be contaminated by Melodie's touch, the old woman pulled her hand away.

"I'm surprised you could be bothered to come home for your mother's funeral," she rasped. "I never held out any hope you'd get back here before they laid poor Gracie in the ground. As far as I'm concerned if you hadn't treated her so abysmally, your mother would have likely found the will to outlive us all."

Too stunned to respond, Melodie gasped at the outrageousness of the accusation. She fought the impulse to bend over double from the impact of the blow. How could a professed Christian be so cruel?

As Cora Linn limped away, Melodie felt other angry eyes upon her. Did everyone present interpret her extended absence as intentional neglect? Could she expect that her lack of tears would brand her an unfeeling monster as well? Her mother had always maintained that just because there weren't any teardrops on the outside didn't mean it wasn't pouring on the inside. Whatever her personal demons, Melodie wasn't about to display them publicly. She supposed that after so much time away she shouldn't have expected to be accepted back into this community as anything other than an outsider.

Cora's verdict that she was a negligent daughter wasn't anything Melodie hadn't already labeled herself. Like the virulent Mrs. Linn, she too suspected that had she only been there to offer support, her mother might still be alive today. Nonetheless the thought of Grace actually confiding her disappointment in her daughter to her outspoken neighbor made Melodie bite her lip so hard it caused a drop of blood to appear.

Buck didn't know what Cora Linn said to upset Melodie, but from her reaction he guessed it shied

away from being charitable. The instant the cantankerous old biddy turned away, he saw the slump
of Melodie's shoulders as she wavered by the dessert table. Unexpected feelings of protectiveness
knifed him. Cursing himself as the world's greatest
masochist, he crossed the small reception area in a
few long strides and slipped an arm around Melodie's waist.

She heard someone behind them gasp.

"What do you think you're doing?" Melodie
demanded through clenched teeth.

"You look like you're about to faint. Why don't
you let me help you to a chair?"

As compliant as a block of marble, she whispered bitterly, "You'd better be careful what you
do. It might be socially precarious to be seen with
me."

Precarious indeed!

Buck had felt temporarily safe in Melodie's
presence only as long as there was some distance
between them. The instant his arm went around her
slender waist, he could no longer allow himself to
pretend that he was anywhere near being over this
woman.

Faking an imperturbability he did not feel, he
asked, "What did old lady Linn have to say?"

"Nothing I haven't thought myself."

Though her face remained a perfect mask of composure, Buck could feel Melodie tremble. The piercing look he gave her coaxed an abbreviated explanation from her.

"Let's just say she wasn't glad to see me."

The good manners Grace had taught him did not desert Buck now. It hadn't been all that long ago when the fine folk of this town had ostracized him. He recalled how Grace and Melodie had both stood beside him, stubbornly refusing to listen to the rumors people circulated about him. Labeled a born troublemaker, he remembered only too well how it felt to be treated like an outsider. It had taken three full winters of shoveling Cora Linn's sidewalk for free before she finally accepted that he wasn't going to slit Grace's throat in her sleep and run off with all her valuables. Not that she had any.

"I've charted these waters before," Buck told Melodie with a wry smile as he scanned the room for approaching sharks. "Why don't you let me help you navigate them today?"

Stiffening against Buck's touch, Melodie kept her back ramrod straight and fought the urge to lean against him for support. How strange that those same neighbors who once labeled him trash were now trying to protect him from her! The hard glances directed at her from among those gathered today were clearly as much for Buck's benefit as for the deceased. Perhaps they thought by casting stones at her, they were showing support for the man she had jilted so long ago.

The irony was laughable. Melodie remembered how long it had taken Buck to penetrate the conservative, cautious nature of those ranchers who clung as tenaciously to their land as to their values. That he had somehow been elevated to a high rank within the church that had made her feel treasured in her youth came as quite a surprise. As she recalled, Buck used to feel about organized religion the same way she had come to regard it. Years of self-inflicted heartache pointed to the likelihood that God was an invention of a patriarchal society designed to keep their members alternately lashing themselves with whips of guilt and shame.

Everyone who came to the services made a point of stopping by to offer Buck their condolences. While many expressed sympathy for Melodie, others used the opportunity to reveal their contempt by ignoring her completely or giving her scornful looks that said they were swayed neither by the fancy talk nor big dollars that had once wooed her away. They did, however, seemed impressed with the man Buck had become. A staunch friend to each and every one of them in an emergency. The son poor Grace never had.

"You sure couldn't tell that blood's thicker than water by the shameful way that girl treated her mother," pronounced Phyllis Brockridge as she added yet another cookie to the neat pile on her plate. Although directed at her equally chubby sister, the comment was loud enough for Melodie to overhear.

Buck knew it wasn't deliberate. Mrs. Brockridge was hard of hearing and thought no one could hear her unless they were standing right beside her. Acknowledging her with a neighborly nod of his head, Buck called the old woman over.

"It was awful nice of you to come today, Phyllis. You were a good friend to Grace, and I know she would appreciate any kindness you could show to her daughter while she's here. You do remember Melodie, don't you?"

A flush of crimson climbed over the woman's white collar at the subtle reproof. "Yes, of course," she said, balancing her plate with one hand and extending the other to Melodie. "So nice to have you home—*at last*."

Melodie thanked the woman for coming. Perhaps being seen talking politely to one of the town's most influential citizens would take some of the chill out of the room. She knew only too well that many people had taken offense at the perception that she had tossed Buck over for a big-shot engineer who whisked her out of state just as fast as he could after their justice of the peace ceremony. When Grace became ill and her only daughter didn't come rushing home for so much as a holiday visit, their disapproval hardened to rocklike condemnation. The judgmental souls who populated the Friendly Valley of Warm Winds would not easily forgive such disloyalty.

That Buck would so chivalrously come to stand beside this traitor in their midst was a surprise to everyone.

Especially him.

Melodie was sure Buck's actions merely confirmed to the churchgoers among the group what an upstanding Christian he had become despite all the many obstacles life had put in his way.

"Lean on me if you're feeling faint," Buck instructed, his voice a sultry command that sapped Melodie of the remaining strength she had intended to use to walk out of this rattlesnake pit. She was secretly longing to take refuge in those strong arms, and her knees wobbled beneath that tempting suggestion.

Pride was all that kept her standing on her own two feet.

"The absolute last thing I want from you is pity, Buck Foster," she whispered angrily,

"That's not what I'm feeling right now," he murmured into her ear.

The warmth of his breath against her neck raised goose bumps beneath the sleeves of her black satin dress.

"Revenge, then?" she guessed warily.

Buck's eyes revealed neither pity nor revenge. Instead what Melodie glimpsed within their golden depths left her quaking beneath the hitherto unthinkable possibility of restoring a relationship with the man she had never been able to stop loving. It was akin to straddling a fault line and hearing the ground rumble beneath her feet. On second thought, being swallowed whole into the bowels of the earth was less frightening than what Melodie was feeling at the moment.

She *had* to stop looking in his eyes. She had to remember where she was and for what purpose.

Melodie strove to remind him thickly, "This is neither the proper time nor place to—"

"Relax, Mel. Relying on me for a few minutes during a stressful time shouldn't compromise you much."

The hint of a smile toyed with the corners of her mouth. "I suppose you're right. And I obviously don't have to worry about compromising my *reputation* with any of the good folk here either."

Buck raised a wicked eyebrow. "We could always give them something to talk about."

"Haven't we given them enough in the past?"

Buck's teasing left Melodie feeling no longer chilled. If this unexpected flurry of brash attention was intended as a diversion to help her get through the next hour of agony, it was working wonderfully. Even in somber garb, devoid of makeup, and wearing her hair in a style befitting a spinster, Melodie felt more aware of her femininity than she had in all five years of her marriage. That she could feel anything but numb at such a sorrowful time was shocking.

It occurred to her that Buck might just be setting her up for some kind of public humiliation. Surely it was too much to expect forgiveness from one whom she had hurt so badly. To simply wish away one's mistakes. To imagine something beautiful coming from the smoldering ashes of their love.

Pulling her eyes away from his, Melodie forced herself to think rationally. For heaven's sake, if a single, respectful arm around her waist provoked such feelings, what would happen if she actually succumbed to the urge to tuck his other arm securely around her, lean up against that granite-hard body and allow another human being to be strong for her for a change?

Like forsaking all reason and attempting to fly off a cliff by simply flapping one's arms, she figured.

Melodie decided that she liked it better when Buck was mean to her. At least then she knew what to expect of him—and of herself.

"I don't know about you," Buck drawled softly into her ear, "but I've had just about enough of polite society as I can stand for one day. What do you say I go get the vehicle and pick you up out front?"

Gratitude flowed from every pore of Melodie's body. "I'd be eternally grateful. It shouldn't take me too long to say my final goodbyes."

Without Buck at her side, Melodie suddenly felt as vulnerable as Lady Godiva. Instead of covering up, however, she lifted her chin proudly in the air and stood her ground as he made his way out the door. Hurt by the reaction of those she'd long considered her friends, Melodie decided if anyone wanted to talk to her, they could darn well take the initiative to approach her.

She didn't recognize the tailored, painstakingly

coiffed woman making a beeline straight for her. Perhaps they had gone to school together. The passage of time certainly hadn't helped her limited ability to remember names and faces any.

The lovely redhead confirmed her suspicions. "You don't know me," she said in a polite, tight voice. "But I think I should introduce myself."

"Were you a friend of my mother?" Melodie asked.

"No."

That single word hung between them, flapping like a red flag hung out to dry on a blustery day. Melodie raised an eyebrow in confusion. Why would someone who knew neither her nor her mother attend the funeral? Intuition kept her from extending the woman her hand. She had a funny feeling she might just withdraw with a bloody stump if she did.

"I'm Judy Roes," the lady stated with a smile that went no deeper than her lipstick. Green eyes glittered with disdain as they perused Melodie from head to toe.

Melodie shook her head apologetically. "Sorry. The name doesn't ring a bell."

Pushing a manicured hand through her hair, the woman responded in a voice so sweet one could have glazed a Christmas ham with it. "I don't believe for a minute that Buck hasn't mentioned me.''

Shrugging her shoulders, Melodie explained, ''We really haven't had much time to visit.''

As Judy Roes chewed on this bit of information, Melodie came to realize that they were the focal point of everyone's attention. It seemed every eye in the room was staring at them. She apparently was the only one in the dark as to this woman's identity and purpose.

''Look,'' Melodie said, jumping to the first reasonable explanation that popped into her head. ''If you're interested in buying my mother's estate, I'm not selling. And certainly not today.''

It was hard to imagine the gall of some people. She liked to think that decency would keep the buzzards from circling for at least a couple of days.

Judy threw her head back as if Melodie had slapped her. Her eyes narrowed into thin cat slits as she hissed, ''I'm not interested in buying anything. I'm Buck's fiancée!''

Chapter Four

Melodie pasted a cardboard smile on her face and ventured a weak, "Congratulations."

What did it matter that the woman had just run a bayonet through her gut? Courtesy demanded a polite exchange before any public execution. She wondered whether contact lenses were responsible for turning the woman's emerald eyes such an impossible color. Better that than jealousy.

Judy pulled a smile tight over blinding white teeth. "I'm truly sorry about your mother. Hopefully it won't take you long to get your things in order so you can move on."

"It might take a little time to get my life in order, if that's what you're asking," Melodie admitted candidly.

The smile affixed to Judy's face didn't reach her eyes. "That's a shame. I was hoping you wouldn't have to stick around here long. After living in that big southwestern mansion we've all heard so much about, it must be humbling to come back to your poor roots."

Melodie bristled at the remark. "Actually it's wonderful to be home," was her only response.

She couldn't imagine how Judy managed to widen that painful smile. Perhaps for the benefit of the crowd Buck's fiancée thought she could mask the undercurrent of animosity flowing between them with those blinding-white teeth.

"Let's just get something straight between us," Judy said in a candy-coated voice, "I'm not about to have you waltz back into Buck's life and stir up trouble for the two of us."

"I wouldn't dream of it," Melodie assured her with an equally bright, albeit tight smile.

Such poisonous personalities didn't bring out the best in her. The thought of Buck actually being engaged to this high-heeled viper set her stomach churning in acid. Of course, Melodie doubted Judy ever showed her betrothed anything other than a sugary sweet disposition.

A flash of candor followed a stab of envy. *Be*

honest. You'd hate anybody Buck was going to marry.

Taking a deep breath, Melodie tried reassuring the paranoid young woman. "I have no intention of interfering in your life. I'm just here to bury my mother. You might consider burying that hatchet you're swinging at the same time. Do yourself a favor and let me put your mind at ease. I'm the last person on earth Buck would ever want to get involved with again."

The smile on Judy's face wobbled for a second. "I just want to make it perfectly understood that he's taken."

Taken what? Melodie wanted to ask her. A turn for the worse? Leave of his senses to get hooked up with someone as hopelessly insecure as you seem to be?

Having lived with it herself for the past several years, she recognized all too well the possessive jealously gleaming in those unnaturally green eyes. It had not only destroyed her marriage but in the end cost her husband his life as well.

His mood swings to paranoia had made him the likeliest target for termination at work when the economy took a downturn. Randall's failure to live within his means coupled with the loss of his "prestigious" job and the overwhelming fear of losing his wife was more than he could cope with. Had he truly considered the aftermath of his decision to put himself out of his misery, leaving Melodie to deal with creditors, grieving parents and the guilt of failing to somehow save him from himself?

Melodie's sigh carried a lifetime of experience in it. "You've made yourself clear. Now let me do the same. I didn't come back home to upset the perfect life you've got planned with Buck. For what it's worth, I truly regret any pain I've ever caused that man. He deserves nothing but happiness, and I honestly hope you're the woman who can give it to him."

Judy put her manicured hands firmly on her hips. "I don't trust you," she stated plainly enough.

"You don't have to. You just have to trust Buck."

With that, Melodie excused herself and made her way through the crowd. As far as she was concerned, those who remained behind were welcome to gossip behind her back and throw every poisoned dart at their disposal. All she wanted to do was go home, collapse and deal with her grief in her own private way.

Buck was waiting for her outside blissfully unaware of what had just transpired between his fiancée and his first love. He was leaning up against his black, polished pickup staring up at the Pinnacles as if searching for answers atop those majestic spires.

"Ready to go?"

Melodie noticed that his eyes were red-rimmed. The sight caused her own eyes to grow moist with emotion. What an immense loss they both shared in Grace's death. Moved by what this man had endured today on her behalf—if only out of respect for her mother—she dared to graze the sharp plane of his face with callused fingertips.

"Thank you," she murmured.

Buck's eyes darkened at such uninvited intimacy.

Surely she hadn't forgotten that he had put on a good show simply for her mother's sake? Melodie dropped her hand apologetically to her side.

"Wait until I get the door open to say that," Buck said offhandedly reducing her heartfelt appreciation of his gift to nothing more than common courtesy.

"I mean it," Melodie repeated, looking directly into his eyes and not flinching from what she glimpsed within their depths. "Thank you."

"You're welcome."

As the sun slipped behind the mountains and

afternoon gave way to dusk, it began to rain again in earnest. Melodie knew the cloudburst would help melt the snow on the ground but doubted whether anything could melt the cold hearts of those who had attended today's funeral. When she said as much, Buck gave her a funny look.

"They're good people, Mel," he told her. "I'd suggest you leave the judging of others' hearts to God."

It came as quite a shock to hear such pious words roll off Buck's tongue. Back when they'd first been thrown together, it had been Melodie and her mother who had tried to convert an angry agnostic to a faith they claimed equalized everyone in the eyes of a forgiving and merciful creator. If not in the eyes of their neighbors...

In retrospect Buck couldn't really blame people for their reservations about him as a young man headed for reform school. He'd been bounced from so many foster homes that he'd come to think of himself as a human Super Ball. Understanding that monetary gain and the thought of looking virtuous to their neighbors was what motivated most of the adults who took him in, he'd dealt with their hypocrisy by doing everything in his power to sabotage the system. And to make himself invulnerable and unlovable in the process.

At sixteen he had run away from a man who used his charges as free labor for backbreaking work and beat them if they dared complain. Buck was halfway across the state in a stolen car when he was caught and brought before the circuit judge. Had fate not brought Grace Fremont into court that day to argue against a parking ticket she felt was unfair, Buck would have likely landed in juvenile hall and eventually in prison.

Something about the way the boy had stiffened his spine against the judge, against the whole world for that matter, moved Grace, who couldn't so much as turn aside a hungry cat or dog let alone a hurting boy with such wary eyes.

"I'll take him, your honor," she'd called out, startling everyone in the courtroom.

Happy to have her take this problem off his hands, the judge had dismissed her parking fine on the spot and offered her a stipend for taking in a ward of the state. Grace turned up her nose at anything that smacked of government entitlement but said if the boy was interested in a job that paid little more than room and board, she was willing to give it a go if he was. Never one for handouts, she expected Buck to work hard for his keep. She'd put him in the bunkhouse not because of the dire warnings her neighbors issued about the young thug she'd taken in corrupting her sweet little girl, but simply because there wasn't enough room in her humble home for another body.

The decision to take Buck in was one she never regretted.

Together Melodie and Buck rode the forty minutes from Dubois to the ranch with nothing but unspoken memories passing between them. They arrived home to find casseroles in the fridge and desserts stacked upon the kitchen table. Bits of masking tape served as labels identifying which neighbors wanted their plates or plastic containers back. Touched by their thoughtfulness, Melodie thought it refreshing to be back in a part of the country where people felt free to come and go as they pleased and no one bothered locking their doors.

"Apparently your hearty appetite is legendary around these parts," Melodie commented. Recalling the displeasure that some of her neighbors had displayed toward her at the funeral, she assumed their largesse was targeted specifically for Buck.

"Don't worry," he assured her. "I'll share."

His teasing smile disarmed her. Out of habit, she grabbed a plate and began fixing him supper.

"What would you like to eat?" she asked.

Buck gave her a puzzled look. "I'm a grown

man and perfectly capable of fending for myself,'' he assured her.

Embarrassed to be caught waiting on him like she had Randall for so long, Melodie bit out a defensive, ''I didn't mean to imply that you weren't. I'm not very hungry myself, and I was just trying to be nice.''

Buck stepped around the table and took the plate from her. His voice was firm. ''You look so beat you can hardly stand on your own two feet. If you don't voluntarily go and lie down right now, I'm going to have to pick you up and put you in bed myself.''

In truth, nothing sounded more appealing right now than being tucked into bed by this strong, thoughtful man, but Melodie wasn't about to be bullied. Even if it was for her own good. Putting her hands on her hips, she glared defiantly up at him.

''I'd like to see you try.''

Buck suspected that making good his threat would be akin to trying to put a hellcat into a silken sack. Even though he was sure to incur several long, deep scratches in the process, it was nonetheless a tempting proposition. Embarrassed at the turn his wayward thoughts had taken, he re-evaluated his intentions out loud.

"Please don't read anything sexual into my concern. I'd do the same for anyone who'd gone through what you have today."

Surprised by the sting of rejection that comment evoked, Melodie countered with more vehemence than she meant. "Tell that to your fiancée!"

"My what?"

She could only assume that confused look on his face was part of his diabolic plan to humiliate her sooner or later. "You know, that *lovely* woman I met at the funeral while you were outside getting the truck. I believe her name had something or another to do with vegetation."

Buck looked at her knowingly. "Judy Roes maybe?" he asked, spelling it out for her to make the homonyms clear.

"More like fish eggs than flowers?"

Choosing to ignore the less than subtle jab, Buck demanded to know, "What exactly did she tell you?"

"Just that you two are engaged and I'm to stay away from you."

The dark thundercloud that crossed his rugged features caused Melodie's heart to skip a beat. Perhaps the woman had overstated her case. "You have asked her to marry you, haven't you?" she asked with false nonchalance.

Buck declined to answer. "Of all people in the world, you have less right than anyone else to ask me that question."

"Fair enough," Melodie agreed solemnly, "but I've got to tell you I don't think she'd take kindly to your offer to put me to bed."

"Probably not," he agreed with a rueful smile.

He had always been a master of understatement, Melodie thought to herself as she grabbed a brownie off a nearby plate and stuffed it whole in her mouth. She hadn't eaten enough throughout the day to constitute a serious snack, but the thought of eating anything more substantial than a mouthful of gooey chocolate turned her stomach.

Licking the remnants off her fingers, she conceded wearily, "I really am tired. If you don't mind, maybe I will take your suggestion and lie down for a little while."

At the moment, Buck was unable to focus on anything other than that tiny spot of frosting at the corner of Melodie's mouth. He railed against his own vulnerability for a woman who had no right to claim even the tiniest sliver of his heart. It had been a tragic mistake to trust her years ago. He wasn't about to make the same mistake twice. His forgiveness lay only in the fact that he'd been too young to resist those bright cornflower-blue eyes brimming with girlish infatuation whenever they were turned toward him.

His heart had foolishly convinced him to ignore the pattern of betrayal his mother had begun when she had abandoned him. Raising a bastard child had presented that old alley cat an insurmountable obstacle to a life of continued carousing. Melodie's past treachery reinforced his low opinion of women in general. And Judy Roes's audacity to claim to be his fiancée when he was so openly resistant to the idea was but another example of how the "fairer" sex was not to be trusted.

In his whole life, Buck had only met one woman worthy of his esteem, and he'd buried her today.

He was relieved when Melodie wiped her mouth with a napkin and padded off in the direction of her mother's bedroom. It amused him to hear her mutilate Judy's name. Though he didn't claim to know much about women, it would have been obvious to a blind man that Melodie was unsettled by Judy's claim. Self-righteous indignation reared its head at the thought. How dare she expect him to sit around eating his heart out in the shadows patiently waiting for her to return someday?

A little belated jealousy on her part was sweet justice indeed.

* * *

Melodie's little nap stretched into hours. She was awakened in the middle of the night by a disturbing dream. In it, the swollen Wind River separated her from her mother. Arriving just in time to watch the bridge between them wash downstream in the raging floodwaters, Melodie plunged into the river fully understanding that her belated effort would likely cost her life.

"Stop!" Grace called out. "Save yourself. Go back. Back to the past. Forgive yourself as I have and follow the song of your heart."

Melodie came to consciousness with both arms outstretched as if trying to embrace the forgiveness of that maternal phantom. Telling herself that strange dream had simply been inspired by all the familiar objects and scents of her mother, she did her best to dismiss Grace's message as poppycock. She could not, however, go back to sleep. After lying in the dark pondering those disturbing images from her mind, she finally gave up altogether and crawled from bed, searching for the light switch.

So as not to disturb Buck in the next room, *in her room,* she corrected herself, Melodie began the painful process of sorting through her mother's things. Putting it off certainly wouldn't make it any easier. In the back of her mind, she wondered if that midnight apparition didn't have this in mind for her when it instructed her to go back to her past and seek happier times.

The question of where all the memorabilia from her room had gone was answered by plundering her mother's bureau drawers. There preserved in tissue paper was every newspaper clipping that marked all of her public achievements. Most recorded her many 4-H and horsemanship awards. Some dated back to high school honor roll announcements, and there was even a stack of perfect attendance citations she'd earned in elementary school. All yellowed with age. They matched the discolored rodeo queen sash folded so lovingly inside the ragged baby blanket that she had dragged around with her everywhere until one fateful day when it had mysteriously disappeared.

Overwhelmed by the priceless treasures of her past, Melodie succumbed to the waves of emotion that swept over her and rolled her over and over again.

Awakened by the sound of crying, Buck slipped from his bed, pulled on a pair of faded jeans and followed the sound to Grace's bedroom. Tentatively he opened the door to discover Melodie huddled in the middle of the floor. Newspaper clippings, ribbons, awards and every childish gift she'd ever given her mother surrounded her. Apparently memories of happier times had released a floodgate of regrets.

Considering that Melodie hadn't cried at the funeral, Buck was startled to see her weeping so freely now. Great grief-racked sobs seemed to tear her very soul from her body. In a secret, petty place in his heart, Buck was glad to see her finally display some remorse. Still, witnessing her suffering gave him a glimpse of living hell hitherto unseen. A giant hand wrapped itself around his heart and squeezed hard.

"Anything I can do to help?" he offered.

Issued from the shadows of a darkened doorway, Buck's voice was a velvet offer. Shaken from her private agony by his overture, Melodie dragged an arm carelessly across her face and mumbled a perturbed, "You can go away and leave me to deal with my grief in my own way."

The prolonged silence following her outburst made Melodie wish she could recall those cold words and replace them with the ones crowding her heart. *Or you could hold me. Catch my tears. And forgive me.*

Stepping into the light of the room, Buck cast a long shadow across her bed. "Too proud to accept sympathy from anybody or just me in particular?'' he asked.

''Sympathy's too close to pity for my taste,'' she told him in a tight voice.

Unfolding stiff legs from beneath her body, Melodie climbed to her bare feet. Though she came only to his chin, an Amazon warrior could not have taken a more combative stance. She raised a fist at him. But rather than trying to strike him, she dropped her hand and slowly opened it to reveal a myriad of pills, some of which they both recognized as veterinary stock.

''I found these in my mother's bedside table. They're *horse* pills.'' Tears glistened in her eyes as she demanded to know, ''Why didn't you call me when you knew she was in so much pain?''

The last thing Buck expected in response to his offer of sympathy was a verbal thrashing from someone who had been so noticeably absent during Grace's final ordeal. Buck wasn't sure Melodie could stand the truth, but he refused to be the one to deny her it. It shouldn't be news to her that more than one hard-pressed rancher purchased his own personal medicine through the local vet claiming that it was for his livestock.

''Grace didn't want you to know. Your mother was too proud to go on Medicare, which she considered nothing more than welfare, and she didn't want to spend a dime of your precious inheritance. I paid for most of her medication out of my own pocket, but toward the end the pain was pretty unbearable and sometimes she snuck a couple of those in on me," he explained.

Melodie flung the offending pills at his bare chest with an animal-like wail. Was he even aware of the checks she had sent her mother so faithfully? The ones Grace stubbornly refused to cash?

Grabbing her by the elbows, Buck held her at arm's length. She doubled her hands into fists and attacked his chest. He suspected that had he not the strength to hold her up, she would collapse beneath the weight of her guilt.

"You should have called me," she sobbed. "I should have been here."

Yes, you should have, he wanted to scream at her. *It was the very least you could have done for your mother.*

Instead he pulled her the short distance into his arms. Cradled against his chest, Buck felt her shake with emotion. Her tears soaked his skin and softened the heart he had wrongly judged to be made of stone when it came to the woman he held in his arms.

"What good would it have done?" he asked,

parroting Grace herself when he had suggested the same thing.

"It would have let her know that I cared." The words were torn from her throat by the bared claws of regret. "I could have told her how sorry I was for disappointing her."

"Disappointing her?"

A choked laugh escaped a throat made tight by guilt.

"Darlin'," Buck continued, "that's something you never did. No matter what, Grace loved without restriction. As far as your mother was concerned the sun rose and set in your eyes, Little Bit. Nobody was any prouder of a child than your mother was of you."

Melodie clung to the undeserved kindness Buck extended her as if to a lifeline.

"You were so good to her," she whimpered. "And to me. And you've been repaid so poorly—"

"Hush," Buck whispered, tipping her chin up to look into his eyes. "You don't have any idea what blessings I received in return for what little I did."

He was referring to more than just the incredible gift of faith that Grace had given him. Far more than the self-confidence she had instilled in him.

How could Buck possibly explain to someone born into a home that promised a lifetime of unconditional love what Grace had given him by accepting him into her home as if he were family born?

"I should have—"

Buck wasn't sure how it happened that he found her lips, but with a sudden dip of his head, Melodie's words were cut off by a kiss that quelled her self-recriminations and opened the door to hope.

Initially his kiss was no more than a whisper upon lips that opened willingly in eager anticipation. Buck deepened it in response to that invitation.

Years ago he had been too gallant to rob her of her virginity. That was no longer a consideration. Still it seemed history was bound to repeat itself. Shock was reflected in Buck's extraordinary eyes as he tore himself away from a situation that had gotten out of hand so quickly. It was akin to a single match setting a wildfire that refused to be contained.

He ran one shaky hand through his shock of dark hair in utter frustration. Not only did he have his own jaded heart to consider, but Judy Roes's as well. Perhaps he was not as involved as she might have led Melodie to believe, but Buck was far too decent a man to disregard the feelings that she had expressed for him. Neither could he freely set aside the deepening of faith which had only solidified those chivalrous views he'd held as a young man. Not without compromising himself.

Then there was Melodie herself to consider. What kind of man would take advantage of a recent widow on the very day she buried her mother? Not the kind who could easily look himself in the mirror the following morning. Feeling a monster, Buck forced himself to release the woman he held so close to his beating heart.

"This is wrong," he said hoarsely.

"Is it your fiancée?" Melodie asked in a whisper that failed to belie the depth of her pain. She had foolishly hoped that Buck's unwillingness to verify Judy's claims indicated lack of commitment on his part. Or at the very least, an overstatement on her part.

"Or is it just me—again?"

She watched the breath that expanded Buck's magnificent chest to full capacity before he responded to the question that she had no right to ask.

"I couldn't ever do to Judy what you did to me," he said slowly. Harshly. "I wouldn't do to a dog what you did to me."

Melodie couldn't bring herself to argue the point.

"Your relationship with her is serious after all then?" she asked, wondering how it could possibly be in the face of their undeniable desire for one another.

Buck saw no need to justify his actions with this woman. Certainly not to disclaim Judy's assertion that they were engaged. He would address his concerns over that particular allegation with her later. In private.

When she dared speak again, Melodie's voice was ragged with emotion. "Would you at least let me explain what happened so long ago? I owe you that much."

Buck's eyes turned as hard and unforgiving as gold that has been tested by fire. In the time since Melodie had left, he had come a long way toward embracing the concept of divine forgiveness. Being nonetheless made of flesh and blood, he was not eager to tear open old scars simply for the benefit of the person who had so cruelly inflicted them. He strode angrily toward the door without giving Melodie a backward glance.

"Save it for somebody who cares."

Chapter Five

So much for making amends, Melodie thought to herself.

While it was certainly true that Buck could have responded with a cruder comment, she doubted whether he could have come up with a more hurtful one. She realized, of course, that she probably needed to clear her conscience a whole lot more than he needed to hear her confession.

Tell somebody who cares, he'd told her.

Trouble was, Melodie didn't know a single soul who did. Intent on molding her into something she wasn't and making sure his needs were met first, Randall had never really been there for her. She had to sacrifice the few friends she had back in

Arizona to move back home, and now that her mother was gone, Melodie was truly all alone in the world. The thought filled her with a rare sense of self-pity.

After her travesty of a marriage to Randall, how could she have been so crazy as to open herself up to another man? Especially one with whom she shared the bad blood of an irrevocable past. She wanted to blame her weakness on the fact that she was emotionally spent. After the ordeal of burying her mother, she had naturally reached out for the comfort he had offered her.

As tempting as it was to cling to that lie, Melodie simply couldn't buy it. In her heart she knew it wasn't true.

Whatever she felt for Buck had nothing to do with sympathy. Not that there wasn't an element of emotional tenderness involved. Indeed, the chemistry between them was as strong, if not even more potent, than she remembered. Buck recognized it, too. And had fled from it in terror. Which, Melodie told herself, would be the smart thing for her to do as well. After the hell Randall had put her through, she was determined never to surrender her independence to a man again.

She knew better than most people the dangers of feeling sorry for one's self. Rather than allowing depression to wrap its tentacles about her, she decided instead to take on her mother's remaining drawers. There was little left to clean out. Mostly just a few favorite shirts and pants faded from use. All the lovely outfits she had sent her mother Melodie found hanging in the back of the closet with the tags still on.

"What were you saving them for, Mom?" she cried out in despair.

Her mother's overly honed sense of frugality had rubbed a raw spot on her heart for years. All said, the pile of clothing and personal items filled but four modest boxes for charity. Climbing back into bed, Melodie prayed her efforts would earn her at least a couple honest hours of sleep.

After his shocking midnight rendezvous with Melodie, Buck could no more sleep than if he had been connected to an IV drip of straight caffeine. Having prided himself for years on being smart enough to learn from his mistakes, he found himself wondering what in the name of common sense was wrong with him. He was glad he hadn't stuck around to hear any lame explanations of why she had run off and married that namby-pamby desk jockey without so much as giving him a chance to object. He didn't have time for any convoluted justification for her actions.

So why then was he driving himself completely insane by playing snippets of the past over and over again in his head?

Besotted fool that he was, he'd actually already bought a ring those many years ago. He'd had it in his pocket when she returned home from college for the holidays. Made desperate from not seeing her for the previous couple of months, he was waiting for her at the door that Christmas like a well-trained Labrador. Dismissing Randall Coleman as another lonely stray Melodie had taken in for the holidays, he hadn't given her sallow-faced companion more than a passing glance before sweeping her into his arms. Earlier he'd strategically placed mistletoe in the doorway that he intended to use to his advantage.

Dragging her beneath it, he'd pressed his lips to hers before she had a chance to utter a word of protest.

"Marry me," he'd implored her.

"Get your hands off my wife!" an angry voice exploded behind them.

Buck would have just as soon forgotten what followed after that: his fist connecting with and breaking the interloper's nose, blood splaying across the living room carpet, Melodie sobbing, Grace yelling and that fool Randall sniveling as he ran from the house vowing never to step foot inside his mother-in-law's home again.

Seeing how Buck's world had blown apart the last time he'd kissed Melodie, he found it hard to believe that he'd voluntarily succumbed to another poisoned embrace. Nor that the feel of the little traitor in his arms was even more wonderful than he remembered.

Punching his pillow, he decided that first thing in the morning he should make an appointment to have his head examined by a team of specialists.

Neither Buck nor Melodie said much over breakfast a few hours later when the sun roused them from restless sleep. Both had trouble looking the other in the eye, as if fearing that direct eye contact might bring on another onslaught of hormonal instability that had left them both feeling wounded last night. Circling one another warily, they hesitated to say anything at all.

''I'm sure you're anxious to get down the road and back to work. Do you need any help packing up?'' Buck finally offered, over his second cup of coffee.

Melodie didn't so much as blink as she calmly informed him, "I'm not going anywhere."

Buck's eyes narrowed.

"What do you mean?" he demanded. "How long are you planning on sticking around?"

"Forever," came her unwavering reply.

Buck jumped up so swiftly from his place at the table that he almost knocked over his plate in the process. "At long last, the truth of why the prodigal has returned comes out. You're just here to claim your inheritance."

It was hard for Buck to fathom that he was being displaced from the only real home he'd ever known. Anger roared through his veins in hot spurts.

"What does it matter to you that while you were off playing the lady of the manor, I was pouring my lifeblood into turning what was once a tumbled-down homestead headed toward the auction block into one of the most prosperous ranches in the area?"

The question was purely rhetorical. He didn't expect or even want an answer. He knew far better than most that life wasn't fair. That was a lesson he'd learned in the cradle.

"Obviously what's a matter of pride to me is just a means to an end to someone like you who's had the good fortune to be born to a mother who loved you unconditionally.''

It didn't matter that she'd never had to prove herself worthy of that love and could do nothing to lose it. In the eyes of the law, all that mattered was that she was tied to Grace by blood alone.

The way Buck was pacing back and forth across the small room reminded Melodie of a caged mountain lion, bleeding and desperate for a way out. Instinctively understanding that anyone opening the door of that cage would be in a very dangerous position indeed, she tried to keep from saying or doing anything to upset him any further. As painful as it was to hear the festering anger in his voice, in her heart she knew that she deserved every hateful word that he flung at her.

''It should only take me a day or two to gather up my things,'' Buck continued, not bothering to hide his bitterness. ''Just let me know when exactly you want me out of here.''

Melodie raised her eyebrows in surprise as she again gave him a single word response.

''Never.''

Buck stared at her as if trying to decide which of her two faces to address. He wasn't sure what she was suggesting. If she expected him to work for her for the meager wages he'd let Grace pay him, she had another good, long, hard think coming. He had remained with Grace out of a sense of obligation and love. He wouldn't work for Melodie if she paid him in gold bullion! His self-respect may have once taken a beating at her hands, but in case she didn't know it, his pride had come back stronger, more indomitable than before.

Assuming it would come as a surprise to her to find out that he had a substantial amount of money stockpiled via his own industriousness, he tried to sound casual as he offered, "I'd like to buy you out. If you're willing to accept a fair down payment and carry the note, I think you'll be pleasantly—"

Melodie held up her hand to cut him off. "You don't understand, Buck. I'm not interested in selling. Whether you or anyone else in this valley wants to accept it, I'm home for good."

"Home!" Buck spat it out as if the mere word on her lips was a desecration. "What could you possibly know of home?"

"I know that as much as you'd like to think otherwise I didn't relinquish it with my marriage," she responded with quiet dignity. "Whatever you may think of me, I want you to know that I have no intention of turning you out. This is your home, too. We have an appointment later today with

Mother's lawyer who wants us both to come down to his office to look at her will. I think we should wait and see what arrangements she made before either of us jumps to any conclusions.''

Buck wanted to shake her. What was the point of having a lawyer tell him what he already knew? That he was no blood relation and as such had no legal rights to so much as a glass of water here. He turned on his heel without saying another word.

The front door slammed so hard behind him that one of Grace's beloved knickknacks skidded off the ledge and crashed to the floor. Melodie bent to pick up the pieces.

"All the king's horses and all the king's men cannot put us back together again," she whispered to the broken glass horse that she held cupped in her hands.

Phillip Hanway, attorney-at-law in general practice, came out from behind his scarred, antique desk to introduce himself to Melodie and exchange pleasantries with Buck. It appeared that the two were already acquainted by name through various community functions. Littered with important-looking papers, the man's desktop was as hard to find as the receptionist missing from the front office.

"Glad you could make it," he said, offering them a seat. In his fifties, the lawyer seemed affable enough and had a nice smile. "First I'd like to offer you condolences on the loss of your mother, Mrs. Coleman."

Melodie nodded in acknowledgment. While they were there, she wondered if it would be a good time to initiate the paperwork to legally change her name back to Fremont.

"Please call me Melodie," she told him.

Mr. Hanway continued, "I have some paperwork to go over with both of you that shouldn't take too long—that is, unless either of you wants to contest Mrs. Fremont's will."

Buck stuck his hand in the front pocket of his jeans and leaned insolently back in his chair. It was all he could do to refrain from putting his work-worn boots up on the desk. Past boyhood experiences had left him leery of anyone associated with the legal system. The will hadn't even been read yet, and this social parasite was already gearing up to take a bigger slice of Grace's meager inheritance by pitting her beneficiaries against one another.

For his part, all Buck hoped for was some sentimental memento to help him remember the finest woman he'd ever had the privilege to know. Life without Grace's kind and patient influence would be colder. Lonelier.

Buck tossed Melodie a disgusted look. If she had left him those long years ago for more money as he was wont to think, would she begrudge him the smallest keepsake? Quite frankly, she was welcome to whatever Grace had wanted him to have. Just knowing that she had acknowledged him at all in her will would mean more to him than he could verbalize.

The lawyer cleared his throat and picked up a thin stack of papers. "You probably are aware that the house Grace left you isn't worth much in its present condition and probably isn't worth the money to fix it up, either. The land, however, has appreciated considerably since you've been gone, Melodie."

That fact didn't surprise her much. Ranch land had been selling for a premium for the past few years, mostly to rich outsiders who wanted to own a real piece of the West and were willing to invest outrageous sums for what savvy Realtors were dubbing "ranchettes." Then, of course, there were millionaires like the ones who owned the place she had managed in Arizona. Often they were overgrown spoiled brats who paid locals a pittance to run the operation for them. Periodically, they would fly in on private jets to show off their dude ranch to bored friends, throw their weight around with the help and loudly complain about how rustic and backwoods the residents were. All said, Melodie supposed that a piece of property along the river would sell for a pretty penny, indeed.

She wanted no part of selling it.

Money wasn't the driving force in Melodie's life. She sincerely doubted whether Grace would want her to put her inheritance on the market before her body was even cold in the grave. Besides, what in the world would she do with herself anyway if she sold out? Buy a big house in town and drive herself crazy with guilt and recriminations most likely. She had few marketable skills outside of ranching. Nor a desire to acquire any. All she really wanted to do was continue the work her mother had started—with similar tenacity, pride and respect for the land.

"I have no intention of selling my home," Melodie informed him coolly. Unless there are so many outstanding bills against it that I can't possibly hang on to it, she added silently.

Buck snorted in derision at her use of the word *home,* and Mr. Hanway looked taken aback at her comment.

"What you and your brother decide to do with

the considerable assets your mother left you is completely up to you,'' he hastened to assure her. ''I simply was pointing out how valuable the land you have inherited has become. In fact, there have been a couple of inquiries that I know of already—''

''We're not related,'' Buck stated, jolted into an upright position in his chair by the lawyer's assumption that they were brother and sister. ''I'm just the hired hand.''

''I don't understand.'' Mr. Hanway shook his head in obvious confusion as he glanced from the handsome couple in front of him back to the papers in his hand. ''The will reads, and I quote, 'I, Grace Fremont, being of sound mind and body hereby bequeath the whole of my estate to be split evenly between my daughter Melodie and my son Buck with the notable exception of money set aside for the church—'''

To my son Buck!

He couldn't believe his ears. She couldn't have given him a greater gift. The fact that Grace had counted him her son meant more to Buck than he could have ever put into words. The dollar figure meant little to him as his heart swelled with the knowledge that she loved him as a mother. That she had made provisions for him to retain his home forever was more than just a generous act. It showed that she understood the agony of being a foundling. It told the world that he was not without family.

Buck saw dollar signs light up the lawyer's eyes as he continued reading. Apparently Grace had somehow quietly managed to grow her modest nest egg into a substantial amount over the years. Though it was news to both of them, they were too stunned by the revelation that Grace had divided her assets equally between them to pay much attention to the numbers Hanway was rattling off regarding her sizable donation to build a new parish hall for her beloved Church of the Valley.

"Mrs. Coleman, if you choose to fight this, I can assure you that precedent has been set in such cases in which the hereditary heir has been granted full rights of—"

"I don't want to fight my mother's last wishes."

Buck was more dumbfounded than Mr. Hanway by Melodie's statement. The little minx was full of surprises. He was reminded of Chief Joseph's famous quote. "I will fight no more forever." Sitting there next to him, Melodie looked far too tired for her years, and Buck felt such a surge of protectiveness that he had to fight the urge to physically shield her from this lawyer's maneuverings.

He wondered if Phillip Hanway might not be feeling the same way. Objectively from his point of view, it could well look like he had duped an old lady and cheated her only child of her rightful inheritance. The thought that others might voice the same sordid opinion of him knotted his stomach inside out. Buck hadn't worked his whole life to overcome a questionable reputation to forfeit it for any piece of property—no matter how attached to it he was.

He wondered how long Melodie had to reconsider her acceptance of Grace's will. The truth of the matter was, this made things a whole lot more complicated for him than had he decided to just up and leave on his own accord. Right now, however, Buck was more concerned about getting Melodie out of this shyster's office and into some fresh air where she could think clearly without anyone unduly pressuring her.

"Is there any possibility that you'd consider contesting the amount of money designated to the church? It is, after all, quite a large amount, and cuts down your rightful inheritance by quite—"

Melodie would hear none of his arguments. While she had no love left for those sanctimonious churchgoers who had snubbed her when she had been most vulnerable, it had been up to her mother how she wanted to spend her money. If Grace had deemed it important to leave her name on a new parish hall, so be it. Melodie just hoped her mother understood that she would likely never darken its new doors.

''There's no need to try to convince me otherwise. Unless Buck wants to contest the tithing to the church himself, I'm ready to sign the papers right now and get it over with.''

Mr. Hanway sputtered his disapproval. ''You understand that there's no need to rush such an important decision. I'd recommend you wait a while and—''

''Where do I sign?'' she asked, impatiently cutting him off.

The determined look on her face gave no indication that she was going to change her mind. Ever.

Buck's mind was reeling. He could imagine the jubilation this unexpected windfall would cause in the parish. Those who had been praying for a miracle would feel their petitions had been answered by God above and the saint who had walked so demurely among them without a hint of the wealth she was accumulating in their behalf. He certainly wasn't going to be the one to contest such a heavenly decree. Still, he had reservations about Melodie signing off so quickly on something that had such a far-reaching effect on her future. While it was true that it was in his best interest to shut his big, fat mouth and simply let her relinquish half of her inheritance to him, Buck didn't feel that was the morally right thing to do. Whatever she had done to him, howsoever he thought she had mistreated her mother, Buck didn't want to be the one to strong-arm Grace's daughter when she was most susceptible to unscrupulous manipulation.

Buck extended his hand and put it gently upon her arm. "He's right, Mel. You should take some time to think about it."

She wheeled on him with blue fire in her eyes. "I told you once. There's nothing to discuss. This is what Mother wanted. For once in my life, I'm going to do the right thing and make sure she gets it."

Chapter Six

An eerie calm surrounded Melodie as she signed the papers. The truth was it would have given her far more pleasure to have seen her mother spend that hard-earned money on herself while she was alive for a few frivolities not to mention such necessities as prescription drugs and preventative visits to the doctor. It sickened her to think of her mother suffering so pitifully with all that money untouched in the bank. As it was, Melodie couldn't help but feel like her inheritance was blood money. She was more than happy to lessen her guilt by dividing it equally in half per Grace's wishes.

She left the lawyer's office feeling like a new person. She had no desire to fight Buck in a court

of law over her mother's will. Relieved that Randall hadn't been there to badger her about protecting
her inheritance and the need to bail him out from
beneath the credit debt he'd run up, Melodie felt
her shoulders loosen from beneath a heavy weight.
It felt good to do what was right for a change instead of succumbing to what others wanted her to
do on their behalf.

She hadn't been surprised that the lawyer tried
to dissuade her from signing papers on the spot.
After all, he stood to make a good deal of money
in a prolonged legal battle presumably protecting
her rights. What perplexed her was that Buck
seemed so intent on fighting Mr. Hanway for the
privilege of pulling the pen out of her hand. Considering that he'd practically had apoplexy earlier
in the day when he'd jumped to the conclusion that
she was turning him out of his home, she expected
him to be thrilled by today's turn of events.

In fact he looked far more troubled than over-
joyed as they took their leave. Melodie hoped he
wasn't laboring under the false impression that she
was jealous her mother had apparently split her
affections between them. One thing marriage to
Randall had taught her was that real love did not
claim such selfish restrictions.

While they had been occupied with legalities

and paperwork, afternoon had slid into evening and put a decided chill in the air. Outside, the fresh air hit Buck full in the face, forcing him to realize that he was not dreaming. He'd gone into this office earlier in the day a belligerent outcast and come out legally recognized as heir to half of Grace's estate.

It had never occurred to him that she would reward him posthumously for his kindness and loyalty. His actions had never been motivated by the promise of any monetary gain. What made it all the more astonishing was Melodie's part in today's proceedings. All these years past he'd comforted himself with the thought that she was nothing but an avaricious gold digger who had thrown him over for someone who could offer her the kind of money and status that he couldn't. To actually have her demand that he receive his fair share of her inheritance was such a turnabout that Buck was having trouble believing her intentions were pure.

It was disconcerting to think that he might have misjudged her over the years. He suddenly wished he hadn't been so quick the previous night in dismissing her explanation of what actually had happened in the past. Maybe, just maybe, there was more to this book than the cover he had slapped on it.

"Let's go someplace and eat," Melodie suggested as Buck opened the door of the pickup for her. "I know Mom would have a fit about wasting perfectly good food in the fridge, but I really don't feel like going back home just yet."

Although there were no establishments in the small town that could boast of being swank, a good steak could be had at the handful of homey little restaurants lining the main drag. They opted for one with a table in the back corner where they could talk without being overheard. Buck thought Melodie looked pretty in the candlelight of the questionable ambiance of the diner. It was as if her decision to sign the papers without further fuss had taken years off her. The taut expression with which she had arrived was replaced by a gentle sense of serenity. Eyes, darkened by troubles upon her arrival, looked suddenly bluer than he remembered.

Lacing the fingers of one hand with the other, she took a demure posture in the seat across from him. Her hands were so like her mother's that it made him pause in reflection. Over the years he had fancied Melodie as nothing but a glorified overseer on that fancy dude ranch in Arizona, doing little more than issuing orders and doling out chores to underpaid underlings. If her hands were a true indication, this woman had not shirked from physical labor herself. It was probably the reason that she was looking so darned thin this evening in a simple cotton shirt and black dress jeans.

In all likelihood, Judy, who took such pride in having her nails done once a week, would be aghast to take a gander at Melodie's callused hands. Buck did a sudden double take when he realized that she wasn't wearing her wedding ring. Had she deliberately set it aside as a sign that she was ready to move on with her life? Surely she wasn't sending out signals that she was interested in picking up their relationship where they had left off, was she? It was far more probable that she had simply misplaced it.

Like his heart.

Having no inkling that Melodie's wedding ring was buried with her mother, Buck didn't bother asking after its whereabouts. Instead he focused in on the other question uppermost in his mind. "Why didn't you contest the will?"

"I didn't want to," she answered simply. Taking a sip of her drink, Melodie hastened to assure him, "Don't worry. I'm not going to change my mind."

"I'm not worried, exactly," he snapped. "I just don't know how we're going to work things out between us."

When she asked what he meant, Buck looked at her like she was deliberately being coy. He set his drink down and gave her a hard look. ''How do you suggest that we share a business and a house without killing each other in the process?''

As it occurred to Melodie that her mother was going to get the last word in yet, she graced Buck with her first completely uninhibited smile since her return. Apparently Grace was determined to mend the fences separating the two people she loved most—even if it meant meddling from the grave.

''It's simple. If you want to sell your half to me, I'll go to the bank first thing in the morning to arrange financing and you can be on your merry way.''

''I don't want to sell!'' Buck sputtered. ''If anyone is going to sell out, you're the logical candidate.''

''Why?'' she almost demanded, knowing that such a question would bring forth a litany of her transgressions. It didn't matter. She wasn't about to sell out just to make Buck's life easier. Having never really gotten over him, she hoped time together would allow her the opportunity to explain her motives to him. He may not forgive her for what she had done, but he might just come to understand why things had happened the way they did.

"And do what?" she asked him instead. "Go back to Arizona? Book a cruise and look for another husband?" She shuddered at the thought. "No thank you. All I know is ranching. The ranch is all I have left of my mother—and my pride. Like it or not, I'm not giving it up, Buck. Face it, the place is plenty big enough for two grown-ups."

Bristling at the directness of the remark, Buck glared at her as their food arrived. Clearly they were at an impasse.

Deliberately disregarding his hostility, Melody cut off a thick bite of steak. Lately the very thought of food made her sick to her stomach, but she felt ravenous tonight. She just hoped she could keep her meal down later. She popped it in her mouth and moaned in pleasure at the flavor. "It's excellent," she informed the waiter who stopped to ask if they needed anything else.

"Just some good old-fashioned common sense," Buck muttered under his breath.

Ignoring the snide comment, Melodie relished her dinner, refusing to let Buck's ill temper spoil a bite of it. Medium rare and seared lightly on the outside, her steak was done to perfection. A baked potato with sour cream accompanied fresh rolls and onion rings. She didn't attempt another word until the last bite of food was gone. It was a nice change to eat a meal she hadn't cooked herself after a twelve-hour day. And it was refreshing to get to eat without having to jump up and wait on someone who carped the whole time about everything she'd done wrong.

After cleaning her plate, Melodie leaned back in the booth and smiled at Buck.

"Ready for some dessert?" she asked.

It was amazing how she could pack away such a meal and retain her figure. Clearly this was one woman who wasn't concerned about cholesterol or fad diets. Buck doubted whether there was an ounce of fat on her lean body. If Grace were here, she'd do everything in her power to fatten her baby up. And offer her extra helpings of the love and tenderness he himself had thrived on at her table.

"What I'm *ready* for is discussing some kind of an arrangement that we can both live with," he told her sharply.

"Just as soon I order a piece of cheesecake," Melodie promised. After such a long time of having no taste at all for life, it felt good reviving her appetite. Having carried out her mother's final wishes, she felt certain Grace would approve.

"What exactly do you propose we do?" he demanded of her when she'd finished eating.

"We *could* do what Mom obviously wanted," Melodie suggested calmly, waiting for him to uncock that skeptical eyebrow before furnishing him with an explanation. "That is, put aside our differences and work together for a common goal."

Buck appeared less than excited by that suggestion. She sighed and attempted to employ the tone that all wise mothers use on headstrong children when they are on the verge of throwing a tantrum in a public place. "All I've got to show for all the years I invested in my marriage and my work is a small herd of cattle. The owners back in Arizona allowed me to graze them on their property as long as I was running the place. I believe you had a similar arrangement worked out with Mom. When I quit, I promised I'd collect them as soon as I got my life straightened out."

Melodie drained the last of her drink. Funny how good everything tasted seasoned with a sense of having done right by Buck and her mother. It was almost as if all her senses had been honed to appreciate every detail of an evening made special by complying with Grace's final wishes.

"I'm making arrangements tomorrow to have

my herd shipped up here. I don't see why we can't share the same range peaceably.''

Buck shook his head as if to check his hearing. Had she really just suggested that they actually forge a business partnership? The only way such an arrangement would possibly work was if they could pretend that the past had never happened and make believe Judy wasn't a part of his life. Professional hypnosis could not induce such forgetfulness in his memory. The hurt of the past and his well-honed sense of honor were too much a part of shaping who he was.

''Sharing the same house won't be nearly as easy as parceling up range land,'' he pointed out dryly.

''We could always paint a white line down the middle of the house,'' Melodie suggested with teasing eyes. ''Just so long as the bathroom is in my part of the house.''

It irked Buck that she was taking this all so flippantly. After all, this was their respective lives she was joking about.

''After being away so long you must have forgotten what a conservative little community this is,'' he reminded her in chilly tones. ''I seriously doubt whether your reputation could withstand the gossip about us living together under the same roof.''

This remark had the strange effect of making her giggle. Buck hadn't heard that sound for so long that it completely unnerved him, sending him back to a more innocent, carefree time of his life. That tingling sound undermined the scowl he was working so hard on.

''Don't worry, Buck,'' she told him, dabbing at her eyes with the corner of her napkin. ''Your virtue is safe with me. I promise not to compromise you in any way that will put you in Erma Mae's weekly scandal column.''

The reference was to the local newspaper's ''Coming and Going'' column. Few if any residents had escaped Erma Mae's scrutiny, making it the first thing anyone read. Melodie was past caring about such unimportant issues. Considering the hell she'd endured these past few years, Buck's concern for propriety struck her as utterly preposterous. She had withstood Randall's paranoia and manic-depressive mood swings that had restricted her social life, not to mention the general consensus that she was responsible not only for her husband's suicide but also her mother's death.

Melodie looked Buck straight in the eye before continuing. ''My guess is you're a whole lot more concerned about what your jealous fiancée is going to have to say about your living arrangements than you are about my reputation, which as we both well know isn't worth a handful of nickels in this community anyway. I've already assured Judy that I'm not out to destroy what you two have together. Why don't you just get married and be done with it? You can move in with her and let me have the house. The lawyer said it isn't worth much anyway, and I do need a place to stay.''

Buck struggled with conflicting emotions. While waves of panic were threatening to swamp his all too rocky rowboat, it seemed Melodie was peacefully adrift in a sea of tranquillity. Her logical suggestion put him in the position of either having to admit that he hadn't proposed at all or marry Judy just to spite Melodie. Not to mention that it bugged the heck out of him to think she couldn't care less who he married. In light of that amazing kiss they had shared, it was utterly maddening.

''I'm not worried about my virtue, your reputation or Judy's perceptions. She is a very understanding lady,'' he said in her defense. ''I'm just uncomfortable with the thought of living under the same roof with you.''

The ice in his voice could replace the cubes melting in his drink.

"That's understandable," Melodie agreed. "I have qualms, too."

Like how she was ever going to be able to concentrate on anything other than her new "partner's" brooding presence, a pair of hypnotic amber eyes that seemed to analyze her every move, and the smoldering embers of their past love that threatened to burst into flames at the slightest breeze. Like how they were going to work out such simple daily rituals as who got to use the bathroom when, and how to avoid bumping into one another in their pajamas.

"Look, I'm sorry if this is awkward for you, Buck. Really I am. But I'm not leaving just to make your life easier. You can either get used to the idea or do something about your own circumstances. I certainly encourage you to consider all your options. Personally I thought you'd be thrilled with what Mom did for you. I know I am. We both get what we want—a home to call our own and the chance to do what we both love for a living."

"Except that we're thrown together again indefinitely," he interrupted petulantly. "And that's one chapter of my life I thought I'd closed for good."

Melodie transgressed proper etiquette by leaning forward in the booth, putting both elbows on the table, and resting her chin in her cupped hands. "Just what exactly is it you want from me, Buck?" she asked point-blank. "I'd gladly change the past for you if I could, but I can't. You've made it perfectly clear that you're not interested in hearing my side of the story, and I can't say that I blame you. For what it's worth, I'm looking forward to working with you. From the figures Mr. Hanway showed us today, I'd venture to say that neither one of us can make it alone. Together I think we could turn this ranch into a profitable venture. Still, I understand that you might be unable to put aside your anger, but if you can't accept what's gone down as an opportunity from heaven above, then you're more than welcome to bail out. Just don't expect me to."

It was a long speech. As a child Melodie had been a veritable chatterbox, but time had worn away any assurance that anyone was paying attention to what she had to say. Over the years she'd come to listen more and talk less. In her opinion, one of the benefits of ranching was the long stretches of solitude in which she attuned herself to the sounds of nature and the voice of reason therein.

"And just what in the heck am I supposed to

tell Judy?'' Buck demanded through clenched teeth.

Ignoring the killing glare leveled at her, Melodie grabbed the ticket out of the waiter's hand as he passed within reach. It was of no consequence to her whether footing the bill hurt Buck's silly male pride or not. Silently thanking her mother for her generosity, she was happy to spend the first of Grace's long-hoarded, dusty dollars on such simple pleasures of living as had been denied her for so very long.

''I'm not sure,'' she responded looking up in the direction of an approaching storm. ''But I'd suggest you think of something fast.''

It appeared a high-heeled tornado was headed straight toward them. Melodie fought the urge to duck under the table at the sight of an expensive purple power suit touching down. Every head in the restaurant swiveled to watch Judy Roes cross the room and zero in on her target. Buck jumped up to offer her a chair. The sweet peck on the cheek he gave Judy did little to displace the wary look in her cat-green eyes.

She smiled politely as she took her seat, gave Melodie a perfunctory nod to acknowledge her presence, and proceeded to focus the whole of her attention upon Buck.

"Where have you been?" she wanted to know. "I've been trying to get hold of you all afternoon."

That Judy was slightly out of breath gave Melodie the impression that she'd been sprinting up and down the street peering into every window in her search for her betrothed. That frantic look on her face gave away more than just her age. She was slightly younger than Melodie had thought from their first meeting, and she was reminded of an age when she herself had been foolish enough to think she could manipulate the universe into making Buck love her forever.

He didn't look particularly happy to be hunted down and publicly interrogated, but Buck nonetheless consented to answer Judy's inquiry with a patented lopsided smile. "We just got out of a meeting with a lawyer," he explained.

Melodie thought he appeared a little too eager about putting her mind at ease regarding the dinner he was sharing with an old sweetheart.

Taking a sudden interest, Judy propped her elbows on the table and leaned forward. "What did he have to say?"

"I'd just as soon talk about this in private," Buck replied, looking around the room. "Why don't you get a bite to eat? I'll drop Mel off home and come right back for you. Then you and I can talk.''

The voracious look in her eyes notwithstanding, Judy maintained that she wasn't a bit hungry. ''And there's no reason for you to drive all the way back into town just for me. Why don't we just let Mel drive herself home, and I'll drop you off when we're done? You can fill me in on all the details on the ride out.''

The juicy details of their up-in-the-air living arrangements were exactly what was making Melodie so eager to extricate herself from what was becoming an increasingly awkward situation. The stab of jealousy she felt at the sight of Buck placing a chaste kiss upon Judy's rouged cheek was a painful reminder that life had been a whole lot simpler when she had been too numb to feel anything. Resurrecting her heart from the dead was pure agony. It seemed some unseen power was intent on making her as miserable as possible until she made amends for all the pain she had caused Buck.

Melodie forced a bright smile upon her face as she took Buck's keys and made a hasty exit.

No matter what her head told her heart, it hurt to lose Buck all over again to someone as obviously insecure and jealous as Judy. The gnawing deep inside Melodie would not let her relinquish her first and only love. Whatever her reasons for the choices she had made, she could never forgive herself for forfeiting that love.

Chapter Seven

By the time Melodie pulled into the driveway, the sun had almost completely sunk from view. Evening's dark mantle was cold enough to warrant starting a fire in the old Franklin woodstove. She was in the process of doing just that when Buck showed up—without Judy. Melodie checked her watch. The time of his arrival indicated that their conversation had been brief. She had a feeling things hadn't gone exactly the way he wanted them to, either.

"Everything all right?" she asked, deliberately turning her back to him and piling more wood in the stove.

"Not really," Buck admitted with a heavy sigh.

Melodie struck a match and put it to the newspaper she had crumpled and placed at the bottom of the grate. Like her feelings for Buck, it didn't take much to fan that small flame into a full-fledged blaze, one that, if not contained, could easily devour everything in its way. Closing the door of the stove she turned to face Buck and saw the stricken look upon his face. Suddenly she felt horribly guilty about reclaiming this house and turning his poor life upside down once again.

It was all well and fine to say they were grownups and capable of leading separate lives under a single roof. It was another to actually live by those words when white embers glowed of their past more hotly than any recently ignited.

"Have you come to a decision yet?" she asked as noncommittally as she could manage.

"Yes, I have."

Not willing to continue unless he was certain of her full attention, Buck waited for Melodie to pull off her boots, set them before the fire, and curl her long legs beneath her in a nearby recliner.

"Since it would be a major hassle for me to drive the twenty miles out here from town every day, I really don't want to move into town."

Releasing the breath she hadn't realized she had

been holding in her lungs while waiting for his response, Melodie strained to keep her face a mask of indifference. It wasn't easy playing the part of a disinterested third party. Part of her still grieved for what she had lost with this man. Despite her best intentions to keep it at bay, jealousy kept rearing its hoary head, reminding her that she was the one who should have married this man and bore his children. It had been her dream from childhood to raise a large family. As an only child, Melodie fancied the thought of siblings who stood up for one another against the rest of the world almost as much as she cherished the thought of making them with a man as passionate and giving as Buck.

Remembering how she had admonished him earlier, she strove to rouse some sincere goodwill for the man whom she had once offered her heart and soul. Just because she had screwed up her life, didn't mean she should begrudge him any happiness he could find with someone smart enough to realize what a jewel he was. And just because the ring that she had worn on her finger had felt more like a rope around her neck, didn't mean things wouldn't work out for him differently. Clearly Judy was crazy about Buck. That in itself bode well for their future together.

"But I don't want anyone getting the idea that the two of us are shacking up, so to speak," Buck added solemnly.

"Of course not." Melodie failed to keep the sarcasm from her voice. "We wouldn't want to compromise your standing with Judy—or the good church-going people of this wholesome little valley. I wouldn't worry if I were you. I have a feeling mother's generous contribution to their church coffers will probably soften their holier-than-thou attitude toward me and anyone cohabiting with me in sin. If your reputation is called into question, you can just tell everyone that you're trying to cast the devil out of me."

Her words underscored the bitterness that had led her so far away from the faith in which she had been raised. Melodie was astonished to see the pity she recognized in Buck's eyes for a born-again heathen such as herself. Years ago she had done everything in her power to loosen the hold that agnosticism had on an angry young man. How ironic that he now was a cherished member of the flock while she was a pariah in the very church that she had been baptized.

She wondered if Buck saw God as she did now—as a stern, missing father figure in her life bent on punishing her for past mistakes. Or did he see God as the kind and merciful creator she had once upon a time described to him so fervently in her childlike innocence?

"Look," she said, wanting to change the subject. Despite the tightening in her chest, she really did want to make Buck's life as easy as she could under the circumstances. "You're more than welcome to build Judy her dream house right here if you want. Wherever you want. Whatever she wants. Believe it or not, I really don't want to stand in the way of your happiness."

At the mention of building a new house somewhere on their shared property, Buck's face took on a pinched look. She couldn't know that he still had the old plans he'd had drawn up for the house he'd planned to build Melodie with his own hands carefully folded and secreted away in the bottom of his desk drawer. Thinking of them once again twisted that old rusty knife in his back. Hurt smudged his golden eyes.

Buck deeply resented this odd turn of events. That his present and former girlfriends both seemed intent in plotting the demise of his bachelorhood was frankly unsettling. Number one, he had never officially asked Judy to marry him.

Number two, it greatly disturbed him that she had told Melodie he had. Number three, he didn't much care for the way Melodie so readily embraced the idea of his marrying someone else.

The least she could do was display some healthy signs of jealousy. Like he had when he'd broken Randall's nose.

Unwilling to carry this charade on a moment longer, Buck made an announcement. "I'm not marrying Judy."

It grew so quiet in the small room that the sound of an ember popping inside the stove reverberated off the four walls and competed with the echo of Melodie's pounding heartbeat. She looked at him in confusion.

"Judy wants me to sell out," he added in lame explanation.

His words held double meaning. But since the abbreviated explanation was intended only to extend to the ranch itself and not nearly so deep as his heart, Buck saw no reason to point out that it was he who had broken off the relationship. Judy was truly devastated by his decision. Having been cast in the role of "the jilted" in the past, he wanted to spare her that added humiliation. If it lessened her pain any to claim she had initiated the split, he wouldn't bother contradicting the local gossip.

"She's convinced some rich out-of-stater or movie star would be willing to buy the ranch for a small fortune. She wants me to take the money, move somewhere with warmer winters and live out our lives in luxury. I tried to explain that even if I wanted to sell out, which I don't, Grace's will provides the other half owner has first rights to the property at fair market value. I told her that I was pretty sure you weren't interested in selling your half any more than I am."

Feeling guilty for being the source of his anguish once again, Melodie felt compelled to nod her head in agreement. She hoped she hadn't pushed him over the edge—like she feared she had Randall. He had assigned her the blame for all his problems before making his final, horrible and irrevocable decision.

"If that was the case," he continued, biting off his words bitterly, "then she 'suggested' that I sell out to you for whatever I could get and walk away a free man in every sense of the word."

Melodie found it hard to believe that Judy would actually ask Buck to give up his lifelong dream of owning his own ranch for any reason, let alone something as ludicrous as an unfounded suspicion that he might still be bound to her on any level. It was no secret to anyone who knew Buck that more than just his sweat had gone into this land. He loved this piece of property as Grace herself had—with his whole heart and soul. Judy was either very stupid or very scared to secure him by ripping him away from his home. The thought of her setting him up as a gentleman of means and teaching him how to swing a golf club made her smile inside.

That smile did not reach her eyes. "Are you sure you two can't work this out?" she ventured in a small, guilty voice.

Buck shook his head and remained mute on the matter. He wasn't about to clarify that the real reason he broke off the relationship was not so much out of concern for where they would live but rather because he was too honorable to continue leading one woman on when he still had such strong feelings for another. And whether he wanted to admit it or not, Melodie's return stirred in him emotions that were not going to go away just because he wanted them to.

He ran his splayed fingers through his hair in a gesture of frustration. Life sure had a way of keeping a fellow off balance. Over the course of a few short days, everything he'd believed had been called into question. After thoroughly convincing himself that Melodie had left him for nothing more than money and prestige, he was dumbfounded to witness her sign over half her inheritance without so much as blinking. Time had certainly made the woman no less a confounding creature than he remembered. The kind of man who took comfort in black and white, Buck was unnerved to entertain the possibility that his was not the only side to the story. Seeing the past from Melodie's point of view might well add troubling shades of gray to his familiar outlook on life.

"All right," he said, giving her a hard look. "Out with it." The confusion that cryptic remark etched upon her features caused Buck to add in explanation, "I'm as ready as I'll ever be to listen to your side of the story. I suggest you make it good because I don't ever want to hear another word of it after tonight."

Melodie knew immediately the story to which Buck was referring.

Their story.

Her blue eyes misted over as her mind drifted back in time. Having waited such a long time to explain herself and beg for forgiveness for her actions, Melodie wanted to make sure she didn't miss anything. A wistful expression flitted across her face.

"Remember the summer I was graduated from high school?" she asked.

"No matter how hard I tried to forget it," he admitted gruffly.

Hoping that the memory of that magical summer might soften the rancor in his voice—and in his heart—Melodie proceeded cautiously. She recalled for Buck how frustrated she had been during those short, golden months. In her mind Melodie had all but thrown herself at him.

"Did it ever occur to you that I held back out of respect for you, not because I was some kind of eunuch?" he growled.

Not wanting to drive him away before she had a chance to say what had to be said, she hastened to reassure him. "I didn't say that. And, no, it truly didn't occur to me that anything other than my own lack of appeal kept you from making love to me."

Buck tried to mask the contempt he felt listening to her misguided account of their shared past. Still, if he had to bite his tongue off, he was determined to hear her out.

"At the time, I actually believed that your troubled background was all that was holding you back from committing to me,'' Melodie explained with a self-deprecating smile at her own precociousness.

Buck wasn't about to argue. His life history certainly supported such a theory, however sophomoric it might be. Indeed, having suffered the ultimate betrayal by his biological mother, he was naturally distrustful of time-honored institutions such as marriage and family. But that Melodie hadn't believed him committed to her struck him as terribly insecure on her part. Not a man who was particularly eloquent with words, he preferred to demonstrate his love with actions. He recalled all the backbreaking labor he'd put in to save for a ring and for a down payment on the home he intended to custom build for her. He hadn't thought Melodie the silly sort who needed sweet nothings whispered into her ear. And, fool that he was, he hadn't believed deflowering her would make him appear more valorous in her eyes either.

''So I decided to take matters into my own hands,'' Melodie reminded him with a self-deprecating shake of her head.

She bade him recall one particular rainy evening in their past—the night she'd announced suddenly that she wanted to go to college. ''What I really wanted was that you would be shocked out of your complacency and demand that I marry you post-haste and have your babies right away.''

Lots and lots of beautiful babies that would have his name and her unwavering love.

In retrospect, she should have realized he would have acted nobly.

"I understand,'' he had said, painfully forcing the words around the heart stuck in his throat.

Of course Buck remembered. Neither time nor willpower alone could erase that fateful night from his brain.

"Let me get this straight,'' he said looking at her as if she were a complete stranger to him. "You're accusing me of *allowing* you to follow your dreams? I can't believe you have the audacity to twist what was the hardest decision of my life into something selfish on my part.''

"No, you were selfless. I was the selfish one,'' Melodie said softly, knowing that in the end, their motives at the time made little difference.

Buck recalled his reasoning with singular clarity. It seemed the very least such a sweet young thing deserved before being tied down to a life of bills, physical labor and mounds of diapers was an op-portunity to spread her wings. Fearing she would ultimately resent it if he tried to clip her wings, Buck knew he had to let her fly back to him on her own accord if their love was to survive the test of time.

By the time she completed her first semester, he figured he would be able to present her with a diamond engagement ring. If at that time, she still wanted to continue her education, he'd support her decision. That would have given him time to get things in order for Grace, pack up his few belongings and follow Melodie back to the only university in the state. He was smart enough to know that it wouldn't hurt him any to pick up a degree either while pursuing his dream of owning his own ranch someday. With Melodie by his side, all things seemed possible.

Her words rang in his head like a noisy gong.

"At the time, I was too proud to admit to trying to manipulate you into a commitment. I hoped a semester away at college would give me an air of sophistication that I was obviously lacking. I was counting on that old adage that absence would make your heart grow fonder and spur your passion to a higher level. I prayed you'd come charging up to the dormitory in your trusty old pickup and ask me to marry you."

Shaking her head in disbelief at her own disin-genuousness, Melodie offered a blunt explanation. "I know it's no excuse, but I was hopelessly stupid as a teenager."

And as a young man, Buck had been idiotically chivalrous. Not that he was about to own up to that fact all these years later. Instead he kept replaying in his mind the scene at the bus stop the day she had left for college. The sky on that perfect autumn day had been as blue as her eyes brimming with unshed tears.

"I love you, Little Bit," he'd whispered into her ear as they parted. "Promise me you won't do any-thing to jeopardize that."

Melodie knew how hard it had been for Buck to say those magical words aloud for the very first time. She'd told herself that knowledge alone would have to be enough to sustain her in the months ahead. She had been, in fact, on the verge of flying in the face of convention and proposing to him on the spot when the bus driver had spit out a long string of chewing tobacco into a can on the floor right beside the gear shift and announced it was time to board.

"I love you, too," Melodie had whispered,

clinging to Buck's neck as if to a lifeline. "If only you knew how much."

So began the long journey to an education that more closely resembled the school of hard knocks than the beautiful ivory tower she envisioned. A place where other men were far less noble than Buck.

"What happened, Little Bit?"

The question drew Melodie out of the bittersweet past and into the painful present. The intensity of Buck's amber-colored eyes burned into her very soul. Though his face had filled out and found its manly grace, his eyes hadn't changed at all. Fifty years hence, Melodie suspected she would be able to recognize this man by his eyes.

"I was foolish—and horribly naive," she managed to say past the tightness in her throat. Now that her chance had come at last, it seemed every fickle word she had ever rehearsed failed her.

Hot tears rose to her eyes. Stubbornly they stuck to her eyelashes. Taking a deep breath of air scented with wood smoke, she attempted to open herself up as quickly as one might gut a fish.

"As you could guess, I was the farthest thing from worldly on the entire campus. Even so, the college boys I met were terribly immature and boyish compared to you. Though I didn't return the attention that they gave me, Randall was more persistent than most. He sat behind me in my geology class and pestered me every day for a date.''

"He was persistent,'' Buck repeated through clenched teeth, urging her to continue.

"Very. To be honest, his tenacity was flattering, but I never did accept a date with him. I told him that I was deeply in love with someone else. The trouble all started when my dorm mate Tina dragged me to a frat party. I was miserable sitting around moping over you, and she convinced me that no harm could come of getting out for an evening of fun.''

Melodie blinked hard and forced herself to go on. "Randall was there. He bought me a drink. I've never been a drinker so when I got light-headed after just one, I assumed it was a reaction to the alcohol. Tina was having a good time and didn't want to leave the party so Randall assured her that he'd get me home safe and sound. The next thing I knew I woke up at his apartment...''

Her voice broke beneath the weight of the guilt she had carried around for these many years. The shame of that night came to bloom in the blush of her cheek.

"…and in his bed."

"Are you trying to tell me that he put something in your drink?" Buck asked in disbelief. Though he'd heard of such things, he couldn't quite imagine anyone stooping so low. Not even someone he had made out in his mind to be the personification of everything he despised.

"I was so ashamed, Buck. I couldn't believe that you would want me back after that. Randall insisted that I was a willing party. He claimed that he was crazy about me. He wasn't above using religion and guilt as a weapon to convince me that we should be married right away. I know it sounds stupid to say it out loud now, but back then I thought I'd go to hell if I didn't make things right in the sight of God."

"Were you pregnant?" Buck asked, searching for a more compelling reason for her betrayal of his love than the one she offered.

"No."

Melodie didn't bother telling him that despite the circumstances she wished she would have been with child. That way at least one good thing could have come from their disastrous union. She saw no reason to tell Buck that she wasn't a mother herself by choice. If loneliness was her middle name, Melodie knew that being alone was just punishment for the errors in judgment she had made in the past.

Years of solitude had made her very good at keeping the company of her own heart.

"You mean to tell me that you just up and married this creep without so much as giving me a chance to forgive you—or kill him, either one?"

Melodie heard the anger in Buck's voice and despised the pleading tone in her response. "I've already admitted to being a fool, Buck. I don't know what else to tell you other than I was scared and young and incredibly stupid."

Buck stood up, effectively eclipsing the only light in the small room. Melodie shivered in his shadow. Standing over her, he reminded her of a marble statue. Cold. Unyielding. Incredibly handsome in his arrogance and skepticism.

"The really sad thing about the preposterous story you've concocted is how very badly I want to believe it," he told her bitterly. His eyes bored into her as if he meant to discern the real truth by peering into her very soul. Though Melodie shivered, she did not waver beneath his scrutiny.

"I've never stopped loving you, Buck," she whispered just as a particularly mean-spirited gust of wind buffeted the tiny house and threatened to sweep her beautiful, heartfelt words away.

Were they to be forever lost in the squall?

Buck looked like a man whose entire world had been overturned without warning. Melodie held out her arms to catch him lest he fall from a high window ledge.

But Buck wasn't about to jump of his own volition. Not the kind to take the coward's way out, he had but one thing to say to this fallen angel before putting her behind him once and for all.

"If that's the God honest truth, you should have had enough faith in *us* to have trusted *me* with the facts when this happened."

With that, he turned and left Melodie alone to battle the ghosts of what might have been with nothing more than the cache of tears she refused to shed in public.

Chapter Eight

Grace had been fond of saying that everything looks brighter in the light of day. As Melodie tossed off her covers and stepped onto the braided rug beside her bed, she certainly hoped her mother was right. Having spent a sleepless night going over her conversation with Buck, she had come to the disheartening conclusion that she really should have left well enough alone. Indeed, unbosoming herself had done nothing but rip open old wounds.

Melodie wondered if fate hadn't written its decree in the stars that she and Buck were forever bound to go through life hurting one another. Doing her best to dismiss such fatalistic thoughts, she padded softly into the kitchen where she had every intention of getting the coffee brewing before jump-starting her day with a shower. With any luck, she figured she could get breakfast on the table and start work before Buck was awake. After last night's debacle, avoiding him seemed the path of least resistance.

Melodie was surprised to discover she was too late to initiate her plan. Standing at the counter with his back to her, Buck had already beaten her to the coffeepot.

"I—I was just going to make some coffee," she stammered over the tripping of her heart.

"Already done. Would you like me to pour you a cup?"

"Thanks, but I think I'll catch a fast shower first," she said. "Please don't feel the need to wait for me before starting to work."

Unable to resist, Buck muttered under his breath, "Honey, I gave up waiting for you a long, long time ago."

Melodie sighed in exasperation. She dearly wished there were some way to take back all the pain she had caused this man who had once upon a time been her best friend. If only the past could be recalled and fixed like a defective car. Or re-written like a bad first draft. Unhappily, she had crossed over this land of regrets so many times that she was familiar with every bruising stick and stone upon it. Reluctant to make the journey again, she resolved that it was time for them both to make peace with the past if they were to ever have a chance at working together in the present.

Her hands went to her hips in a gesture of pure frustration. "You have to know that I didn't intend to bring up old hurts again last night. I just thought you would want to know why things happened the way they did. That's all. If you and I can't get past that, if I have to watch every single word I utter around here, living together is going to be more trouble than it's worth—the ranch notwithstanding."

Melodie paused a moment to rub the throbbing pulse on either side of her eyes. She felt unusually tired for so early in the morning. "I don't know about you, Buck, but I really need this arrangement to work out."

His eyes softened at this admission. His voice was husky and raw as he grudgingly acknowledged. "We both do."

He had, in fact, done his best to explain that very same thing to Judy just last night. Having left both Melodie and him equal shares in her ranch, Grace knew full well that this was a sink-or-swim proposition. Half a working ranch simply couldn't function properly. If they were going to make this work, they had to work together. Otherwise they were destined to drown together.

"We both know what your mother was up to," he grumbled, glaring at Melodie as if it were somehow her fault.

Melodie smiled weakly.

"Mom never did hide the fact that she wanted you as a son-in-law. In light of her will, I guess neither one of us should be so surprised that she intended to see that the two people she loved the most reconcile their differences."

Buck shook his head at such female caginess. There had never been any question whether Grace had been infirm in mind in her last days. But as much as he wanted to honor her final wishes, he nevertheless couldn't help resenting her interference from the grave.

Reading the hard expression on Buck's face, Melodie addressed the image of her mother within her mind's eye. *As good as your intentions are, it's not going to work, Mom.*

Even if Buck could someday manage to forgive her, Melodie just didn't think he was the type who could ever forget. Instead of bringing two wayward lovers together as she had obviously hoped, Grace had only managed to make things worse.

A rasping sigh derailed Melodie's train of thought. Buck jammed his splayed fingers through his hair. "Why don't you go take that shower now?"

How dearly she wished the door to the past could be shut as easily as the bathroom door that she locked behind her. Having lived with a man who'd struggled just to drag himself out of bed every day, Melodie was impressed with the mere fact that Buck had managed to use the shower earlier without waking her up. That he had actually taken the time to wipe it down blew her away. Simple courtesies meant a great deal to a woman used to cleaning up after her husband in every respect.

By the time she finished showering, changed into sensible clothes and downed a cup of strong coffee, Buck was already hard at work. Melodie found him whistling a tune in the barn saddling up a pair of horses. She tried to remember just how long it had been since she'd heard that happy sound.

Recalling how his whistling used to fill her with a sense of utter contentment, Melodie took a deep breath of clean mountain air and greeted the rising sun with a heart made lighter by the tune on Buck's lips. Knowing she was now far better prepared to deal with anything he might throw her way, she stepped inside the barn and addressed him in a cheerful voice.

"Where do you want me to start?" she asked.

Buck looked up from tightening the cinch on his horse's saddle to gaze at the woman standing in the doorway. Framed by soft pink rays of the breaking day, she was as heart-stoppingly beautiful in a Western striped shirt and jeans secured at the waist with a leather-tooled belt as any Paris fashion model. A pair of leather gloves, red bandanna and black cowboy hat completed the thoroughly Western outfit. The only thing overtly feminine about what Melodie was wearing was a pair of gold hoops hanging from her ears. That she made such a pretty picture in overtly plain clothing made him wonder about why women wasted money on the latest trends.

You can start by looking a little less attractive, he was tempted to tell her. Instead he replied more gruffly than he intended, "If you're talking about making yourself useful, you could start by grabbing a pitchfork and start mucking out these stalls."

If Buck thought she was going to turn up her nose at such a lowly, distasteful task, he was mistaken. Melodie reached for the implement without complaint. Feeling suddenly light-headed, she reached out a hand to steady herself against a nearby stall and chastised herself for skipping breakfast again. Tomorrow she vowed to get up even earlier and put something more substantial in her stomach than toast and coffee.

Inside the stall, a magnificent chestnut mare whinnied her concern. Melodie guessed the mare would foal within the month.

Stroking her nose, she reassured the animal. "Don't worry, beauty. Buck just uses that loud bark to hide that big soft tender heart of his. He wouldn't hurt a flea let alone a pregnant lady such as yourself."

Oblivious to Melodie's sudden wooziness, Buck grunted his displeasure at the offhanded compliment. He would rather die than admit how her words took the chill off the morning air.

"Any particular reason you're saddling two horses?" Melodie asked with feigned nonchalance.

Buck didn't look up. "Since I've already fed the stock, I thought you might like to take a ride with me and check the old place out, see what, if anything's, changed around here."

Melodie was delighted by the prospect. This prolonged time afoot had left her feeling antsy, off balance and out of sorts. Shrugging off her earlier faintness as the product of stress and lack of food, she grabbed the pitchfork with renewed enthusiasm.

"I can't think of anything I'd like better," she admitted, determined to hasten their departure by making short work of his request that she muck out the stall.

It had been a long time since anyone had shared Buck's workload, and he was surprised how well the two of them actually functioned together. No longer the childish magpie chatterbox he remembered, Melodie had developed into a remarkably strong woman. He was flat out amazed at the amount of work she put forth without so much as a word of complaint. He'd worked men who had less avidity for purely physical tasks. Once again he found himself wondering if he hadn't been mistaken about the nature of her managing position on that fancy dude ranch.

Distracted from his own work, he wished he could find some way of repressing those haunting flashes from the past in which he glimpsed Melodie with straw in her hair from the times they'd playfully wrestled in this very barn. Her indictment last night couldn't have been further from the truth. But he had solemnly vowed that when the right moment came, it would be special.

As a young man, Buck hadn't bought into the concept of organized religion at all. Still, despite his troubling doubts about God, Grace somehow had instilled in him a fierce sense of right and wrong. Now that he was fully grown and had miraculously come to embrace his faith, he couldn't very well regret his decision not to take what a naive Melodie had so willingly offered those many years ago. But it was hard not to feel remorse. Buck reminded himself that taking the high road sometimes lengthened the trip, but the destination was worth the extra miles.

Tempting shortcuts often only led to dead ends.

It saddened Buck to see Melodie harboring the same doubts about God that he once had. He hoped the years hadn't turned her back on the religious convictions with which she had been raised. Since they were going to be living together, he wondered if he could coax her into attending church with him and hopefully finding solace in God's loving ways.

Resolving to work on the concept of forgiveness himself before preaching to another, Buck sternly reminded himself that brooding over the past was just as dangerous as indulging in present day fantasies. If he wasn't careful, he just might upset their fragile working relationship and his recently found spirituality by succumbing to the urge to take Melodie in his arms....

From the whistle on Buck's lips to the smell of leather in the tack room to the feel of a saddle under her, Melodie took delight in the discovery that everything old was new again. Perhaps it was true, she thought, that one must first lose what is most dear to the heart before completely understanding how truly precious is the gift called home.

Riding the range with Buck, Melodie realized just how much she had missed the land of her birth. Looming in the background, the towering spires of the Pinnacles were but a prelude to the majesty of the Tetons hidden from view by the rugged terrain. The scent of pine perfumed the air, and the heavy burden of snow upon the ground was finally giving way beneath spring's persistent determination. In the lower valley, patches of brown were already starting to show through snowy drifts. Still sluggish in its present icy state, the Wind River promised rushing floodwaters to come as surely as Melodie's heart pumped blood of its own accord.

She longed to kick her horse into a full run and race Buck across the meadow as they had in days of old but knew it wouldn't be prudent to risk her mount's neck in the accumulated drifts, many which were deceptively deep. Tilting her hat back on her head, Melodie drank in the panoramic view as they took their time riding the fence line. The improvements made to the property were abundant and easy to see. The old homestead might well be falling down as Lawyer Hanway had so bluntly put it, but the ranch itself was in the best shape she could remember.

"You've done a lot," Melodie commented laconically.

"I've been busy while you were away," was Buck's equally succinct response.

Had he not been so entranced by the way that her hair captured the sunlight in its strands of gold, he might have been tempted to expound upon his endless labors. As it was, it was all he could do to try to force back the desire to reach out and free the rest of her shining tresses from beneath that cowboy hat and test its silkiness against his callused hands. Bewildered by his weakness, Buck forced himself to tear his gaze away from her to the property they were surveying.

Melodie could well understand the pride in his eyes as he took in the land stretching before them as far as the eye could see. Wolves and bears still claimed this land as their home. At best, human stewards kept the wilderness at bay and learned to accept that man-made improvements upon this earth were as temporary as the wooden crosses that once upon a time marked pioneers' graves.

Their pace as they traversed the land was leisurely. More at home on a horse than anywhere else, Melodie enjoyed every step of the journey. Unhurried by the hands of a clock, they wandered through an enchanted land where past, present and future were forever intertwined.

"Oh, Buck, look!" Melodie cried out.

She pointed to a weathered tree house in a cottonwood beside a wide spot in the river. An old rope swing hung from a low branch. Here on lazy summer days one might be tempted to taunt the river with bare toes stirring the water's surface or perhaps take a death-defying plunge into the deep pool where prized rainbow trout were known to lurk in the shadows. A living remnant from Melodie's youth, the tree house had been here when her mother had brought Buck into the family. More often than not, when the chores were done—or occasionally avoided—she could be found here immersed in a stack of library books that took her to far, faraway places. Here she wept over the agonies of adolescence. Here Buck had carved their initials into the bark of the tree and proclaimed their love for eternity.

Melodie directed her horse toward the tree house and, upon reaching her destination, leapt from the saddle. Ground tying her horse, she raced for the swing, taking care not to slip on a patch of ice. It had been ages since she'd done anything so utterly frivolous and carefree. Feeling the wind in her hair as her body arched to the heavens, she heard a strange sound emanating deep in her belly and bubbling upon her lips like champagne spilling from the bottle. Melodie wondered if her laughter sounded rusty from lack of use.

Buck found her uninhibited behavior wondrous and so very reminiscent of the girl he once loved with all his heart. Moved by the magical sound of her laughter, he wondered what had happened over time to take such a vibrant woman and turn her into but a shell of what she once was. Why he suddenly felt the need to help her discover her old confidence and zest for life again was beyond him. Perhaps it was merely his heart's way of healing itself after all this time.

"Push me, Buck!" Melodie called out in a breathless gasp.

Much to his amazement, this hardened rancher found himself climbing out of the saddle to do her bidding. Her mirth was so contagious he couldn't seem to help himself. Grabbing the outside edges

of an old wooden board that sufficed for a seat, he
hoisted her high in the air.

Her squeal of delight echoed off the mountain
walls.

"Unders!" Melodie teased using the old ver-
nacular. She knew full well that running under this
particular swing would mean plunging headlong
into the frigid river below. Remembering a time
when they were young and foolish enough to accept such a dare for the sheer exhilaration of feeling life in every fiber of their bodies, she kicked
her boots toward the gathering clouds overhead
and squeezed her eyes shut.

Up, up, up...

Down, down, down...

Just like falling in love all over again...

The thought almost caused Melodie to lose her
balance as she remembered how Buck used to
make her feel as if her feet never touched the
ground at all. Once upon a time she had laughingly
referred to the malady as Buck Fever. Too late, she
realized that coming here was a bad idea. Revis-
iting the favorite haunts of her youth stirred up old
emotions that were better laid to rest.

Too much time had passed. Too much hurt endured.

Melodie dragged the heels of her cowboy boots in the softening earth.

By the time she came to a halt, her hair was loose about a face flushed with unexpected emotions. Watching her smile fade before his eyes Buck was surprised at the depth of his longing to keep it affixed upon her face. The sad, dark cloud overshadowing the yearning in Melodie's eyes made Buck want to reach out across the span of time and enfold her once again in the safety of his arms.

If only… he thought to himself.

Watching her gaze linger on the initials carved in the tree trunk then wistfully trace her way up the board steps leading to the tree house itself, he wondered if Melodie, too, was remembering the stolen moments of their past. Many were the tender kisses shared within the questionable privacy of a fortress made of cast-off lumber. Many the dreams shared. It was a special place for both of them.

As if afraid he might glimpse her very soul in the windows of her eyes, Melodie dropped her gaze to the ground. Slowly, she made her way back to her mount. Back to reality and adulthood and feet-firmly-on-the-ground sensible-type thinking.

If only… Melodie thought, expelling her regrets

with a deep, troubled sigh. Climbing back in the saddle, she turned her mare toward a nearby pasture where she had fences to mend.

Years and years worth of them.

Chapter Nine

Though few things are more tedious than mending fences, Melodie far preferred having something so arduous to do with her time rather than brooding over things she couldn't fix at all. Indeed, the physical requirements of keeping a ranch up and running provided her with just the kind of healing she needed most. Whether restringing sagging barbed wire, moving irrigation pipe, working the stock or rubbing down a horse in need of a good rest, it felt good to be working for herself for a change. Preserving her own heritage meant far more to Melodie than any paycheck she had ever received as an employee. The clear blue sky above, the fresh, pine-scented air and feel of her own sinews stretched taut beneath the surface of her skin was medicine enough for an aching spirit that had forgotten how to pray.

That she and Buck fell so easily into the rhythm of a work routine that allowed them to coexist peaceably was a great relief to her. Though a strong undercurrent of caution still ran silently beneath their daily interactions, Melodie was grateful to discover that their cease-fire was holding up better than her own resolve. Every day the flimsy bridge connecting her past and future was threatened by a flash flood of emotions in her present.

It was only after her husband had been laid to rest that she was able to admit her desire to do more than simply make amends with Buck. At least subconsciously, she knew she had come home hoping to see if an old flame might be reignited.

If in her youth, pride had been an obstacle too momentous to overcome, in maturity it was proving an even greater hurdle. Though Buck was making a concerted effort to remain polite and positive, Melodie felt one-hundred percent certain that he wanted no part of any reconciliation with her beyond what was necessary to advance their shared business concerns. Nevertheless, she couldn't help fantasizing that the quiet evenings they shared belonged to a husband and a wife, each content in the tranquillity of the other's presence. Once Melodie came to the decision to allow Buck his reticence rather than trying to ease the awkwardness of their silence with endless chatter, meals became a part of the day that she genuinely looked forward to. She greatly preferred shared solitude over having to listen to Randall complain about her cooking, her looks, her lack of education and anything else of general interest that he could think of to pummel her self-esteem.

It was a pleasant change just spending time with someone who didn't vacillate between manic-depressive mood swings.

To Melodie the breaking of bread symbolized a healing that was long overdue as Buck offered the blessing each day, giving thanks to God for the generous bounty of the land. That deeply ingrained habit of her youth brought Melodie's callused working hands together in prayer once again. How she longed to truly believe that a higher power actually heard and cared about her petitions to renew the cherished relationship she had so clumsily misplaced.

They both carefully avoided any reference to Judy Roes. Plagued by feelings of guilt for so perniciously disrupting Buck's life once again, Melodie pitied the woman who had come so close to actually getting a commitment from him. After all, Buck wasn't the kind of man who gave his heart away easily.

Told by numerous foster parents what a bad boy he was, Buck learned early on that he was unlovable. More than one significant adult in his life had endorsed beatings by reciting that old adage about sparing the rod and spoiling the child. No matter how hard they tried, it seemed no one was capable of "beating the devil out of him."

Melodie had done her best to reverse that kind of twisted thinking by smothering Buck with love and positive affirmations. Ultimately, however, her decision to follow her conscience and marry Randall instead of heeding her heart undid everything she had done to build up Buck's sense of worth. Melodie knew that having taken the supreme risk as a young man of offering his heart to another only to have her turn her back on him, he had given up any silly fantasies about romantic love and vowed to never allow himself to feel so deeply ever again.

And so it was that their conversations were limited to such general topics as the weather and specific concerns about the ranch itself. Buck was relieved to discover that Melodie had a more modern attitude toward running a business than her mother had. He had tried broaching the subject of upgrading their antiquated irrigation system with Grace before, but, with all due deference to her memory, the woman had been notoriously cheap. Her answer to any equipment problem had been to buy some more duct tape or a bigger roll of baling wire.

At least Melodie didn't cringe at the amount of money he thought necessary to invest in their mutual future. Perhaps as long as they avoided any painful references to the past and focused entirely upon the welfare of the ranch, he came to the conclusion that they just might be able to make Grace's ridiculous plan work after all. As much as he hated to admit it, Buck found he truly enjoyed Melodie's company. Not only was she a hardworking partner, she was also bright and funny in an offbeat sort of way that frequently caught him off guard and compelled him to look at things from a different perspective. Despite his determination to remain immune to her charms, Buck was drawn in by her gentle strength and unnerved by the sorrow in her eyes.

Every chance he could, he did some little thing to help renew her broken spirit.

Those little things did not go unnoticed or unappreciated by Melodie who in the month she had been home found herself tearing up over some small kindness extended to her. Like the morning she awoke to discover Buck shoveling off the walk solely for her benefit. Snow the last day in April was not an altogether freak thing, but the amount accumulating on the ground was record breaking. Taking in the glory of each unique flake dancing across the sky, Melodie didn't mind the inclement weather. She had quietly adapted in the month she'd been home. In fact, she much preferred the cold of Wyoming to the blistering heat of the Arizona summers she'd gladly left behind.

It had started snowing just before sunrise and showed no signs of letting up. Anxious to repay his kindness in turn, Melodie fed and watered the stock and helped Buck load some hay into the back of the truck. Surreptitiously she reveled in the fat flakes that drifted so softly to the ground. When they stopped falling, she knew the weather would grow cold once again, but it always fascinated her how relatively warm the temperature remained in the midst of it actually snowing. She liked the way that snow covered up everything ugly and rusted and made even the most barren landscapes pristine. And she blushed when Buck caught her testing a couple of snowflakes on the end her tongue.

Clearly amused that she would take such enjoyment from something he considered a burden, he employed his most jaded voice in telling her, "I'll give you less than a week before you get tired of the snow again."

"I'll show you," Melodie replied with a rare grin.

It was, in fact, all she could to keep from spinning around and around in dizzying circles yelling "Freedom!" to the echoing mountaintops. Wet and heavy, such a snow bent budding trees to the ground in supplication making them look like a convent of nuns in white habits offering their prayers in unison. Seized by a sudden childish impulse, Melodie formed a perfect snowball between her gloved hands, and when Buck wasn't looking, took careful aim.

"You've just forgotten how to have fun is all," she chided, knocking his cowboy hat squarely off his head.

Taken completely by surprise, Buck vowed revenge. Without giving thought to the repercussions, he plunged his hands up to the wrists in the soft snow and felt the cold seeping beneath his gloves.

Melodie took off running across the corral. She squealed as a white missile whizzed by her head. Doubting whether Buck had missed her on purpose, she didn't stop to gloat about his poor marksmanship but kept right on heading toward the safety of the front door. She recalled a time when she was in junior high and Buck had so infuriated her with his teasing that she had tricked him outside in nothing but his long underwear. She then proceeded to lock him out until he promised not to retaliate against her.

If her legs didn't fail her, she could hopefully employ the same trick again.

"Oh, no you don't!" he hollered behind her.

Though she thought she felt his breath upon her neck, it was neither lack of speed on her part nor Buck's superior physical ability that kept her from reaching the front door first. Rather, the soles of her boots slipped out from under her and she went buns first into the fresh snow. Luckily it was already deep enough to cushion the impact.

Standing over her prostrate form, Buck wasn't quite sure whether he should strike a victorious or concerned pose. Melodie lay on the ground so still that he worried the wind had been knocked out of her.

"Are you all right?" he asked.

"Help," she mumbled, holding a shaking hand out to him. "I think I might need to see a doctor."

Buck's heart kicked like a mule against the inside of his chest. Chastising himself for his part in such juvenile antics, he bit back an adultism about how Melodie should have known such tomfoolery was bound to lead to disaster. About how they both were far too old to be acting so childishly. About how terrible he felt about allowing her to get hurt.

"Do you think you broke anything?" he asked, extending her his hand.

The next thing he knew Melodie pulled him face first into the snowbank beside her. He came up like a snowshoe hare popping out of his hole, sputtering indignantly and wiping a clear spot on his face out of which to glare at the devious, little mischief maker who had tricked him.

"Just your cantankerous mood," she giggled, and seeing the thunderous expression on his face added in a smaller voice, "I hope."

Buck lunged for her.

Too quick for him, Melodie rolled away, resting at last upon her back several full turns away. Squinting up at the dim sun overhead, she stretched out her arms and embraced the falling snow. Feeling as if she had somehow been magically transported inside a miniature snow globe, she couldn't imagine that no two were truly alike. Just like people. In a voice breathless with the sheer exuberance of life, she beckoned Buck to join her in making snow angels. Waving her arms about her in the snow, she urged him to forgo the responsibilities of being a grown-up for one brief, magical moment.

''Your angel's missing something,'' he grumbled.

Crawling over to kneel beside her, he added his own artistic touch to her body sculpture: a pair of devil's horns.

She showed her disdain by stuffing a handful of snow down his back.

He rubbed her face in the snow until she begged forgiveness.

This was the old Melodie that Buck remembered so well. Laughing, teasing, grabbing hold of life tightly and refusing to let go lightly. This was the imp who had bewitched him so many years ago and would not yet release him from her silken bonds. Buck was thankful to catch a glimpse of that old self behind the somber mask she donned at the start of every day.

Taking off a single glove, Buck brushed the snow from her face with warm and gentle fingers.

The tender gesture was her undoing. Blinking, she peered into a face as open and honest as any she'd ever been privileged to love. Putting both hands on either side of that rugged face, she attempted to fix the crystalline beauty of the moment in her memory forever.

As he studied her, Buck's eyes softened. The mingling of their breath turning to steam in the cold air was the only thing separating them. Melodie's eyelids fluttered shut. Her lips parted expectantly.

As gently as the snow falling from heaven above, Buck's mouth came down upon hers.

"You are still so beautiful," Buck whispered, all traces of teasing gone from his voice.

Fearing that he could see nothing but ugliness inside her, she sucked a gulp of air into lungs burning with pain. It was hard to breathe with an ever present rock of shame pressing down upon her lungs.

"Stop it," she told him, her words heavy with hurt. Squirming beneath him, Melodie sought escape from his piercing eyes. "No woman likes to be made fun of like that."

Buck refused to let her up. Instead he pinned her hands to the snow and compelled her to look at him. "What *did* he do to you, Little Bit," he demanded to know, "that changed you so?"

The tears that rose to her eyes were hot enough to melt the snowflakes clinging to her eyelashes. Too proud to cry in public, Melodie was dismayed at the tears welling up inside her and falling down her cheeks. Personally she thought Buck had every right to leave her frozen to the ground by this crystalline trap of her own making.

"The real question you should be asking," Melodie choked out, "is what I did to him. What I do to anyone who makes the mistake of loving me."

Buck wiped away her tears with a tender, callused hand.

Melodie felt as if he were attempting to brush away the flies covering the gentle essence that once upon a time had been her soul. Lying there unable to run from the memories, she recalled the disparaging remarks that her husband had said to her. Fearing that she would leave him if she ever realized what a weight he was dragging her down, Randall worked hard to convince his wife that nothing about her was right. If ever Melodie had looked in a mirror and been happy with what she saw, her husband made sure she saw a reflection that was haggard and drawn.

Seeing the light in Melodie's eyes dim with the pain of remembering, Buck felt driven to examine the wound such a simple compliment had exposed to the elements.

"What are you talking about?" he asked, removing his hands from her wrists. Rather than striking out at him as he feared, Melodie wrapped her arms around his neck and spilled her tears into the fur-lined collar of his coat.

Certain that the goodness in him was the only thing blinding him to the evil in her, Melodie squeezed her eyes shut. How could she admit to another human the shortcomings that had not simply curled her soul around the edges but killed it at the very core?

Melodie struggled to find the right words. It didn't matter how painful the process. She could not in good conscience allow Buck to be hurt again. "Just don't ever let yourself get too close to me again," she warned cryptically. "It could be dangerous."

"What are you talking about?" Buck demanded to know. His voice was so rough and impatient that Melodie sensed he wanted to shake her.

Opening herself up like this was hard. Too hard in that it meant sacrificing what little respect Buck had left for her. Gathering up her courage, she did her best to sever any lingering emotional attachment he might have for her.

"People who get too close to me don't seem to live to regret it," she tried to explain.

Buck's forehead wrinkled in confusion as Melodie continued, her voice a faraway echo in her own ears. "Surely you of all people have made the connection between me and the fact that that those close to me seem destined to die before their time."

Buck's growl would have frightened a less courageous soul.

"That's nonsense, and you know it."

"Tell that to Cora Linn," Melodie whispered, deliberately mentioning the old family friend at the funeral who had vocally and publicly held her responsible for Grace's death. A shudder racked her body, and her teeth began to chatter from the cold both inside and outside her. "Tell it to the friends Randall left behind. And while you're at it, would you mind mentioning it to Randall's parents, too?"

"Gladly," he told her, cupping her head between his hands and refusing to let her turn away. "You're not responsible for anyone's death. Who do you think you are to question God's will?"

"The person who found my husband's body swinging from the rafters."

The admission came from someplace so deep inside her that the words almost sounded torn from her soul.

Buck stiffened. He hadn't known that Randall's death had been a suicide.

"He left behind a note blaming me for driving

him to it,'' Melodie continued dully. ''If only I'd been a better wife, maybe I could have helped him to—''

An expletive best expressed Buck's opinion on the subject. If there had been any question about the story Melodie had related earlier about Randall's dubious character, this final act of cowardice cinched it. He flinched beneath the sudden knowledge that Melodie had been carrying around such a heavy load of guilt.

''Listen to me,'' Buck commanded. ''If your husband was foolish enough to take his own life, it wasn't because of anything you did or didn't do. It sounds to me that a superhero couldn't have toted the emotionally overpacked baggage that miserable excuse of a man brought to your marriage. Something was wrong inside him, Mel. Nothing you could have done would have fixed it. A man is responsible for his own life. Don't ever forget that. It's something Grace reminded me of whenever I got to feeling like a victim.''

Gratitude flowed through Melodie like warm water. Buck's compassion and understanding was salve to a soul she had thought dead. Considering their past, she had expected him to take pleasure in the discovery that she had failed Randall as a wife. She had thought it likely he would laugh at her. Worse yet if she had seen pity emanating from his eyes.

"Beating yourself up won't help any, either," Buck assured her gently. "It certainly won't bring him back. You've got to let go of this and accept that death isn't your fault."

"I don't know how to let go of it," she admitted. In a secret part of her heart, she worried that the shame was all that was keeping her together.

Moved by his own guilt for the remonstrance he'd placed upon her for neglecting her mother, Buck could think of but one way to help her begin the healing process. How he was going to bring her back to faith in herself and her fellow man was beyond him, but he knew he couldn't live with himself if he didn't at least make an effort to do so. Reaching back in time, he recalled what Grace had done for him when she found him in a similar spiritual void.

"I'd be honored if you'd accompany me to church this Sunday," he said, sounding as if his collar were buttoned too tight.

Melodie's laughter was cold and hard. And as biting as the sky emptying itself of the last of its snowfall.

"Do they have a special pew for sinners like me?" she asked.

"You could always sit with me," Buck suggested, ignoring the sting of her sarcasm.

"Wouldn't that be rubbing salt into Judy's wounds?"

Buck shook his head sadly. "I suppose part of the reason things didn't work out for us is that Judy and I don't see eye to eye on religious issues. Truth is, she isn't much of a churchgoer."

Melodie hated to admit that she was no regular, either. Since leaving home, it felt like God had simply abandoned her to a life of penance and hard work. Bitterly, she confided that such a God wasn't anyone she felt like spending much time with.

"Well then, I won't push you," Buck said, forcing a tight smile upon his face.

Rolling off her, he pushed himself off the ground and rose stiffly to stand over her. Melodie was reminded of some magnificent Zeus sheathed in a layer of white powder.

"Right now, I suggest we get you out of those wet clothes before you catch your death of cold."

It had been an expression her mother had often used, and hearing it made Melodie feel small again. Small and foolish.

She didn't dare pull any more tricks as she meekly took Buck's hand and felt herself pulled through the air and set upon wobbly legs. Oddly enough, she felt suddenly lighter. It amazed her that exposure of her deepest, ugliest fears had not caused Buck to turn away in disgust. That he had reached out to her in friendship and support was incredibly humbling.

And healing.

If *he* could absolve her, was there a chance that Melodie could ever come to forgive herself? The thought gave her hope as Buck held the front door open and she was greeted by the warmth of an old Franklin stove and the possibility of a truly merciful God.

Coughing, Buck wrestled with the very demons he had worked so hard to exorcise in Melodie. Her words echoed over and over in his mind like the refrain from a haunting song. He threw a bale of hay so hard against the side of the barn that it shook the tack hanging there. It was no use. He could no more banish her words from his memory than he could erase the image of her lying upon the snow-covered ground looking like a broken china doll. Memories tugged hard at his conscience.

I never stopped loving you.... she had said so earnestly not so very long ago.

Unable to admit the same to her that cold, hard

night, Buck had turned away, leaving Melodie alone with her own anguish. As much as he wanted to believe those sweet words, he knew better. Hadn't his own mother issued such false assurances of her love the day she dumped him off at the local Department of Social Services? Was it any wonder that he had such difficulties getting his mouth around the very word *love?* Had his own stubborn tongue been freer with the sweet platitudes that he assumed Randall had so liberally dispensed those many years ago, he couldn't help wondering whether Melodie would have been so quick to forsake him.

Her revelation about her husband's suicide was as disturbing as her reasons for marrying the loser in the first place. Those pretty blue eyes had held no sign of duplicity whenever she offered up another piece of the puzzle of what had gone wrong between them. That she truly might not have tossed him over for the first college boy promising a glittering future far away from this ramshackle old homestead was more than just a little disturbing to Buck's peace of mind. It was all well and good to feel sanctimonious if one never had to glimpse the world from someone else's eyes. Indeed, ever since Melodie had returned home and stirred up old regrets, Buck felt the earth trembling beneath his feet.

Trying to make sense of bits and pieces of their conversations from the past few days made his head ache. Buck certainly couldn't imagine anyone as strong as Melodie taking physical abuse from anyone. Seeing her as the shell of her former self, he wasn't so sure, however, that she hadn't been the victim of emotional abuse.

The notion sent a chill through a body already numb. Soaked clear through to the bone from rolling around in the snow like some pubescent boy who didn't have any more sense than what God gave a young stag, Buck was reluctant to admit that he was freezing. Cross with himself for allowing Melodie to draw him into such silly adolescent horseplay, he trudged toward the front door of the house. Hopefully a hot cup of coffee and a warm fire would not only help get his thoughts in order but also stave off a case of pneumonia.

Whatever had possessed him to kiss Melodie on that soft bed of snow was beyond all logic. Cursing his weakness as a man, Buck shook his head in bafflement over his own conduct. He liked to think he was of at least average intelligence and above average morals.

He most certainly didn't consider himself the

kind of man to spy on an unsuspecting woman caught in a state of undress.

Buck's high-born principles were sorely tested when he found himself in just such a position and discovered that he could no more have moved from his spot than had he been planted there in concrete. Coming in from the cold, he poured himself a mug of coffee and took up temporary residence in front of the wood-burning stove in the middle of the living room. As he warmed his backside, he became aware of the sound of the shower running. He noticed that the bathroom door was ajar, probably in an attempt to keep the steam from peeling any more wallpaper from the walls. From his unique vantage point, he had a partially obstructed view of Melodie clad in only a towel stepping out of the shower.

Before he diverted his gaze, Melodie caught Buck's eye. Years of being neglected and mistreated by her husband had left Melodie vulnerable to any man's attention. And Buck wasn't just any man. He was the exemplar to which she compared every other male and always found them lacking. The man she couldn't forget. The man she loved for a lifetime—and would love beyond the grave if such a thing were possible.

If he came to her now, Melodie knew that she would not refuse him.

Through the steam, Melodie watched Buck cross the distance separating them in a few short strides. She steadied herself by putting one hand upon the cool porcelain of the freestanding sink.

Inwardly Buck struggled with what he wanted to do and what he knew to be right. He wanted to assure this wounded beautiful woman with words and actions that she was not the cause of anyone's death. To take what she was offering and make her his own. To turn fantasy into reality at long last.

Buck stood at the doorway a long moment grappling with himself. How easy it was to be virtuous in solitude; how very difficult when face-to-face with delicious temptation. He understood all too well that the magic of this moment was complicated by the past.

Nothing could change it.

Neither of them would ever be able to forget it.

Submitting to sensual pleasure under such circumstances was surely a prescription for calamity. Buck wondered what kind of a man would take advantage of a woman after she had professed herself in such a vulnerable state.

A man like Randall was the response that echoed in his ears.

That thought alone gave Buck the strength to reach out and grasp the doorknob with a trembling hand.

Click.

Without a single word, he closed the door between them as softly as a whisper.

He could not know that Melodie would interpret his high-minded behavior as yet more proof of her failings as a woman. Waiting to hear his footsteps fall away, she sank to the floor in self-loathing, holding one end of her towel over her mouth to stifle any sobs that might give her away.

Had she merely imagined that predatory look in his eyes? Had his hand trembled when he reached for that doorknob out of fear? Or disgust?

Dropping the towel, Melodie dragged herself to her feet to stand before the mirror, an objective judge of her appearance. Blotchy from crying, her face did seem fuller than when she had arrived. Too much good food she assumed had made similar changes noticeable in her angular form.

Beneath the layers of wounded pride, a seed of indignation sprouted. She may not win any beauty pageants any time soon, but she was not altogether physically repugnant, either. Undoubtedly it was what Buck saw inside her that had shut that door between them. Considering that he had not turned away when she had confided the worst of her sins to him, she could only assume that it was Buck's newfound sense of religion that was holding him back. Melodie had to give him credit for not being a hypocrite like so many she knew who professed their godliness in church and sinned like crazy behind the preacher's back.

She didn't know how they could go on living like this—torn between the past and the present, between denial and desire. Staring hard at her naked reflection in the mirror, Melodie vowed to leave Buck to the comforts of his holier-than-thou attitude. Feeling cheapened by the incident, she told herself that she wouldn't exchange another minute of her time trying to make herself worthy of a man who found her so completely unappealing.

Chapter Ten

"As long as you're living under my roof, you will go to church with me and honor the Lord's day...."

How clearly Melodie remembered the weekly battles her mother had waged in an effort to save Buck's soul from eternal damnation. Standing at the juncture of the same fork in the road this bright Sunday morning that she had once so fervently urged Buck to take was an irony that was not lost upon her. Church was becoming as volatile an issue between Buck and her as it had once upon a time been between him and her mother.

Secretly, Melodie admired his tenacity. That Buck didn't seem dissuaded in the least by her repeated curt refusals over the past several weeks to his invitations to attend services with him was indeed a testament to his commitment to the cause. And though Melodie was loath to admit it, she was more than just a little jealous of the sense of serenity that settled around Buck whenever he returned home from church.

Serenity was definitely something that had eluded Melodie since she had left this modest mountain haven. And while coming home had indeed given her an innate sense of being where she wanted to be, she dearly missed the sense of belonging to a community that embraced her as one of their own. With the exception of going grocery shopping and opening up an account at the local lumberyard, she was practically living the life of a recluse.

"Aren't you at least interested in stopping by out of curiosity to check on the progress being made on the new parish hall?" Buck asked in a studied offhand way.

"Just because the new church addition will have my mother's name on it and is being purchased from the proceeds of her will doesn't mean that I'd necessarily be welcome there." Her words crackled as dryly as autumn leaves beneath the boot. It was a tribute to Grace's memory that building had begun, pending paperwork notwithstanding. The estate was a simple matter with nothing owed against it. Grace owed no one nary a penny but the undertaker. As the will stood uncontested, there was nothing to slow down construction.

"I suppose not," he assured her with an equally wry tone, "but it couldn't hurt any, either."

Melodie tried to tamp down the smile that rose to her lips. The last thing she wanted to do was give this man the least little encouragement on this particular subject. She couldn't help but believe Buck had asked the good Reverend Solans to stop by and personally thank her for Grace's benevolent contribution. Not that she didn't appreciate the gesture, whatever its impetus.

"What with the unusually warm spring weather, you'd be surprised how far along the building is," he continued deliberately ignoring what appeared to be a grimace twisting her lovely features. "In the six weeks since you've been home, the structure is up and drywalled, thanks to the large number of volunteers and the fact that the foundation was already completed last fall through donations. About all that's left is the finish work."

At that, the ill-disguised smile Melodie wore broke completely loose. How very like her mother to demand elbow grease on the part of the parishioners in exchange for her generous contribution. Not that Melodie thought it was such a bad idea. Experience had taught her that true pride in ownership came not simply through the acceptance of gifts from benefactors but rather from the contribution a person invested of himself in making an investment a personal mission—whether it be in purchase of one's own modest home or in an asset that enriched the lives of the entire community. Melodie was grateful that her mother had the foresight to raise her with such a healthy philosophy. Had it not been for Grace's sensible homespun wisdom and a deep belief in her own ability to make her life count, Melodie suspected she might well have been the one dangling from the same self-tied noose her husband had used to end his life.

"You know we could always use another hand," Buck added. "And having worked with you over the past month and a half, I'd lay odds that the two of us could single-handedly have the whole thing finished in less than a week."

Melodie thought it a funny compliment, but seeing as she wasn't going to receive one for her beauty and charm, she graciously accepted Buck's appraisal of her work ethic. In truth she found it more affirming than anything he could ever say about her clothing or hairstyle. The prospect of working with him on a project that meant so much to her mother clearly appealed to Melodie on more than one level.

Still, just remembering the last time she had stepped inside that church was enough to twist a knife in her gut. If in speaking her mind Cora Linn had intended to inflict the kind of wound that refused to heal, she'd certainly accomplished what she had set out to do. Weeks later, the injury was as yet raw to the touch.

Melodie shook her head no to indicate that she wanted no part of a work detail that included rubbing elbows with the same people who had snubbed her in a time of such great emotional need. Lately she had taken to thinking of some of the local parishioners as prayer terrorists—people so twisted in their thinking that they actually prayed for evil to befall others. She'd dismissed their generosity in bringing food over after the funeral as being more about following accepted mores than a genuine show of support.

"You will, of course, come to the dedication," Buck pressed. "It's set for the twenty-seventh, just two weeks from today. Your mother would want you to be there."

How do you know what my mother would want?
she was tempted to ask.

Suspecting that it would only open up a discussion on faith that she would just as soon avoid,
Melodie refrained from asking that question aloud.
Besides, for all her resistance to stepping back inside that little church, she knew that Buck was
right. Nor was she the type to run from her problems. It was silly to think there was any way to
keep avoiding all her old acquaintances forever.
She might as well get it over with sooner than later.

The thought of showing up unannounced for
work detail was far less intimidating than making
an appearance at what was sure to prove a strained
dedication ceremony. At least this way Melodie
figured she could defend herself against the slings
and arrows of her enemies with a hammer if need
be. Also no one could say she hadn't contributed
anything more than part of her rightful inheritance.

Tipping her chin up in that determined way of
hers that Buck had come to so admire, Melodie
conceded. ''All right. I'll go with you today. For
Mom's sake, I'll put in my community service time
on this project. Just don't expect me to endure
some long-winded sermon. You can join me in the
hall after the services if you want.''

Buck started to open his mouth to argue but

thought the better of it. Getting this woman any-where near the church was a big first step. As much as he regretted the way some of the parishioners had treated Melodie upon her return, he also knew that judging the entire congregation by the actions of a few was grossly unfair. If she would just give them another chance, Buck suspected her old friends would rise to the occasion. Remembering his own struggle with acceptance in this conser-vative little community, he simply smiled and as-sured Melodie he'd be there as soon as services let out.

Expecting him to put up more of a fight, Mel-odie was disappointed Buck hadn't given her any reason to defy him. She downed her morning cof-fee, hot, black and bitter, before heading off to get ready for church. Dismayed to discover her favor-ite pants were becoming snug around the middle, she deliberately chose an old faded pair of jeans in hopes that Buck would chastise her and thus give her an opportunity to dig in her heels and renege on her promise.

''Ready to go?'' was all he said.

Her mother would have been horrified to see her go anywhere near a church in anything other than a properly ironed dress. Buck was wearing a dark tailored suit that hugged his impressive frame and emphasized a football player's set of shoulders. Noticing that he carried his own work clothes in a neatly folded pile, Melodie assumed he would change out of his suit after services. She stubbornly refused to do the same. She told herself that it didn't matter a whit whether it galled the congregation that she would pound nails during services. She hoped the noise would awaken some of them from napping during the sermon. She hoped it might stir a conscience or two.

Springtime in the Rockies is always spectacular. Melodie and Buck both enjoyed the scenery on the way to town that pleasant Sunday morning. The last of the snow was melting, and the soft color of emerging grasses was contrasted against a sky more vibrantly blue than any painter could ever hope to capture. Attempting to avoid any pretense for an argument, Buck occasionally looked over at Melodie and smiled reassuringly.

She scowled back, hoping outwardly to maintain her antagonistic attitude in the face of such a lovely morning. Inwardly she appreciated Buck's gesture of support. Old habits die hard, and she was having a difficult time looking at her scuffed boots without feeling guilty for the way she was dressed. Her mother had been a stickler for appearances, especially when it came to church. As the miles ticked by, Melodie found herself remembering the many times she and Grace had traveled this same road every Sunday of her childhood. She recalled the white dress, matching anklets and frilly hat that her mother had bought for her first communion. It seemed a lifetime ago that she had been so young and so eager to participate in a ceremony marking the way to adulthood. How she longed a return to a time of such innocence and joyful expectations.

By the time they pulled into the parking lot in Dubois, Melodie was not just regretting her choice of attire but also her very presence here. Her heart skittered nervously in her chest at the prospect of running the social gauntlet yet again. Though it was bound to make some difference that her mother's name was on the impressive addition adjoining the original structure of the church, Melodie suspected she would remain the community pariah until the day she died. Would they refuse to bury her in the same section as her mother, citing lack of church attendance as a reason to stick her in the agnostic section of the cemetery?

She doubted their censure would continue on into the next life. Still, she was somewhat surprised that Buck had agreed to live with her, even on a platonic basis, for fear of hurting his reputation. That he actually reached out and took her hand into his as they entered the building caused moisture to rise to Melodie's eyes. How could such big, strong hands be so gentle? So incredibly sensual?

Turning her head away so that he could not see her tears, she made a big deal of inspecting the new construction. Simple in design, the progress that had been made was indeed impressive. Melodie made a point of entering the addition through a separate door rather than stepping over the threshold of the church itself. There was room enough to seat the entire congregation comfortably at tables for any given occasion. Modern and serviceable, the kitchen facilities boasted a walk-in freezer and matching oversize refrigerator. Large enough to cook several turkeys at the same time, the convection oven also touted a smooth advanced surface that promised to boil water in an instant but not to burn flesh, an especially handy feature for a community facility where curious children were plentiful.

That Grace had never owned anything half so nice in her own home galled Melodie. Bitter feelings of resentment welled up inside her. It was all well and fine that her mother had left such a charitable contribution to the community, but would it have hurt her to have spent a portion of her savings on herself? In Melodie's opinion there was a fine line between being frugal and wearing a hair shirt, a concept whose merit had always eluded her.

From the sounds of the music drifting through the building, it appeared Mrs. Wardwoot was still the organist. Though not particularly accomplished, the woman's strength was in her volume and the charity of her ever willing spirit.

Funny how the refrain of that familiar old hymn resonated in the chambers of Melodie's heart.

"Are you sure you wouldn't like to go in with me?" Buck asked softly, squeezing her hand and causing her to look directly in his eyes of burnished gold.

Strangely enough Melodie found that she did, but remembering what she was wearing had her head shaking no. Perhaps God would be glad to see her in church regardless of what she was wearing, but she suspected the congregation would have a less charitable reaction. When Buck released her hand to take his leave and join in the assemblage next door, she felt completely adrift in a sea of loneliness. Melodie had to bite her lip to keep from calling him back. Surely, asking him to miss services on her account would be taking advantage of his goodness.

It wasn't at all hard to imagine what it would be like to accompany this hardworking man to church each Sunday. She could envision their little family filling an entire pew themselves. While not immune to fidgeting, they were nonetheless a handsome crew. The boys would look like their father, and the youngest, Daddy's little girl and the apple of his eye, would be snuggled safe in Buck's arms. Was there any use denying that it was the very place Melodie yearned to spend the rest of her days?

No more use than in pretending that it was ever going to happen.

As the sound of the entrance hymn faded away, Melodie shook her head to clear it of such useless fantasies. If she hadn't been able to conceive a child with Randall, what made her think anything would be any different with Buck?

She decided to channel her thoughts down a more productive route. As tempting as it was to grab a hammer and disrupt the services next door, Melodie opted instead for a quieter paintbrush. Spite was a poor reason to antagonize the congregation any more than necessary. She opened a can of enamel, then positioned a stepladder beneath an unfinished windowsill.

Stirring that paint seemed symbolic of stirring up all the memories that had settled to the bottom of her consciousness. The more Melodie stirred, the more the color came to the surface. When at last a lovely new shade emerged from her efforts, it was impossible to separate colors out. Old and new blended together, as did the present from the past.

Some psychics told the future by reading tea leaves. Melodie wondered if she was the only woman on earth trying to make predictions by stirring a quart can of enamel. The fumes of which were unusually strong, she might add, feeling suddenly light-headed. Her foot slipped upon the rung, and she struggled to maintain her balance. The last thing Melodie remembered was dropping the entire can on the floor when everything suddenly went black....

When she woke up, the first thing Melodie saw was Buck's face hovering over her. The concern etched in worry lines upon that rugged, handsome face was almost enough to make the tumble she had taken worthwhile. Embarrassed and fretting about the mess she had made, Melodie hastened to reassure him that she was fine.

"I'm just glad the carpet hasn't been laid yet. It's a good thing I didn't volunteer my services earlier," she joked weakly, feeling an egg-size knot on the back of her skull. "I could have put the whole project back by months."

Buck squeezed her hand.

Hard.

When he spoke, his voice was tight with emotion. "Don't worry about a little spilled paint. Right now I just want you to focus on getting better."

Looking around her, Melodie realized with a start that she was no longer at the church. Rather, she was tucked neatly into a hospital bed, surrounded by four clinically white walls that felt like they were closing in on her. Apparently she had given herself a concussion when she had fallen and knocked herself out.

Embarrassment consumed her. Randall's voice taunted her from the grave.

Couldn't she do the least little thing right?

"I hope you didn't call an ambulance," she told him. Even the short trip to transport her from the church to the hospital would be an exorbitant expense unwarranted by such uncharacteristic klutziness.

"No," he said quietly. "I brought you here myself."

In fact, he had carried her into the emergency room in his own arms bellowing orders to everyone on staff. He didn't mention that to Melodie. Nor that finding her bleeding and unconscious upon the floor, he had lost his temper back at the church, yelling at friends and neighbors alike over their egregious behavior toward her. Or that thinking her dead for an excruciating moment, he had felt his own heart stop beating.

"I feel so silly," Melodie admitted, thinking all the fuss unnecessary. For the life of her she couldn't figure out why she was hooked up to an IV.

"I didn't think to open a window to let the fumes out," she added apologetically.

Buck seemed distracted. Melodie wondered whether he had even heard a word she had said. She closed her eyes and wondered what kind of medication they had given her. Having been married to a man addicted to antidepressants that did him little good, Melodie was worried about what drugs were pumping through her system. What she really wanted to do was rip that IV out of her arm and check herself out of the hospital.

"Why didn't you tell me?" Buck asked, his voice a ragged tear from a throat clogged with emotion.

"Tell you what?" Melodie mumbled.

Impatience flickered in his golden eyes.

"About the baby."

Melodie looked confused. "I don't know what you're talking about."

"Don't play games—" he started to say, but the look of genuine mystification on Melodie's face stopped him.

She didn't know.

A heartbeat later understanding dawned in Melodie's eyes. Her hands immediately went to her stomach in a protective gesture.

"Did you say *baby?*"

She said the word as if testing a miracle upon her tongue. Was it possible that she was pregnant? Melodie recalled the last time she'd been with Randall. They so seldom touched anymore that Melodie had been taken aback and moved to pity when her husband broke down and admitted that he was a failure. Looking back on it, clearly sex had been her husband's way of trying to prove himself to her one last time. That their union had been strained and sad apparently had no effect upon conceiving a child.

Had Randall unknowingly left her with child? That would certainly explain the bouts of nausea and dizziness she had been experiencing lately. Not to mention the puffiness that she'd simply attributed as weight gain from actually sitting down to eat three meals a day for a change. She'd been too busy grieving and dealing with the conditions of her mother's will to pay much attention to her body.

A wave of elation carried her away. Having thought herself barren, Melodie had given up on the possibility of ever being a mother. She had resigned herself to having nothing more than a herd of cattle to give meaning to her life.

"A baby?" she repeated.

Looking into Buck's stricken face, she was shaken by a terrible possibility. Had she miscarried when she fell? She couldn't believe God would be so cruel to give her the child she had always wanted only to snatch it away even before she knew of its existence. She reached for Buck's hand for strength.

"Please tell me that I'm pregnant."

The quaver in Melodie's voice was enough to make his throat tighten painfully. That Buck had actually thought her capable of deliberately hiding a pregnancy from him seemed suddenly absurd. It was excruciatingly clear that she knew nothing of her state of health. Silently blaming the doctor who had brought her condition to his attention for not being there, he was sorry he'd ever made mention of it. A health professional was a far better candidate to break such news to a woman than an old flame who, through a strange twist of fate, just happened to be her business partner.

"I'll get the doctor," he said, rising.

Terror turned Melodie's face an even paler shade. She dug her fingernails into the palm of Buck's hand. "No," she implored. "You tell me."

Reluctantly Buck sat back down. "I can only repeat what the doctor told me," he warned.

Nothing in his life of professed bachelorhood had prepared him for this. So recently widowed, Melodie could have any number of responses to the news that he felt honor bound to deliver. He knew that single motherhood wasn't the easiest job in the world. Grace herself often attested to that fact. And having a mother himself who resented his place in her universe, Buck wasn't quite sure whether Melodie would be saddened or relieved by the possibility of a miscarriage.

He winced at the pressure of her nails pressed against the palm of his hand. It was nothing compared to the pressure she was wielding upon his heart. How long had it been since he'd opened that battered organ up to empathize completely with another human being's pain? Too long he gathered by the way his heart swelled up like a balloon inside his chest.

"You are pregnant," he said, pushing a stubborn lock of hair from his vision. "I assume you didn't know."

Melodie nodded numbly in agreement as if she couldn't quite believe it yet herself.

"They're running some tests, and we don't know the results yet," Buck continued.

He didn't want to be the one to tell her that there was a distinct possibility that she might have lost the baby in the fall. Worried what yet another loss would do to her health and mental well-being, he felt an overwhelming surge of male protectiveness course through his veins. Suddenly, he wanted nothing more than to scoop Melodie into his arms and assure her that he could make everything better.

But he could no more lie to her now than he could when they were kids.

And certainly not when she was looking at him as if staring into the face of an angel heaven-sent to personally deliver her a miracle and defend her against dark forces. Before the news of her condition had a chance to sink in, he hastened to add a word of caution.

"You have to understand that there is a possibility that you might have lost the baby when you took that nasty fall back at the parish hall."

Melodie's heart tumbled in a free fall of emotions.

But she smiled at Buck bravely.

The last person in the world to shy away from reality, Melodie simply refused to consider the possibility of losing the baby growing so secretly beneath her heart. She was willing to commit to whatever it took to save the life of this innocent. If that meant spending the rest of her pregnancy in bed, so be it. If it meant hanging upside down for the same length of time, she would do that, too. And if it meant reconciling herself to God through prayer and penance, she would sell tickets if that's what it was going to take.

"A baby," she said again, squeezing Buck's hand as if to make sure she wasn't dreaming. "Wouldn't Mom be thrilled?"

Buck nodded and smiled at the image it conjured. The joy lighting up this woman's beautiful face was enough to dispel any doubts he may have initially had about whether Melodie would want a baby at this time in her life to remind her of the husband who had so emotionally battered her. Though not a man easily given to judging others, he was proud of her. Many a woman overwhelmed by the prospect of raising a child all on her own had decided to eliminate the problem legally and do away with the infant's life before it had a chance to open its eyes to the world. Its tiny heartbeat could easily be kept a secret from those who might speculate as to the mother's promiscuity and question the baby's patronage.

Buck bristled against such ugly pettiness. God had best help the man who slandered Melodie in front of him. In all likelihood, he knew that any vile remarks would not be directed at him but rather *about* him. He could only imagine the number of rumors that would fly from barrooms to bedrooms in and about the small town of Dubois.

As a man who had come to love peace in his maturity, Buck wasn't so sure he could put aside his old tendencies to use his fists if anyone was ever stupid enough to slap him on the back and make some off-color remark implicating him as the father of Melodic's child.

At the thought, sadness came to settle on his shoulders like a pair of heavy black wings. He wanted to be the father. Desperately in fact. The realization socked him squarely in the solar plexus.

Had fate and his own stubborn pride not interfered, he would have been, too. By all that was right, the baby Melodie was carrying should have been his. Should have imprinted his genes upon future generations. Should have carried the seal of his love and guidance into a world distinguished by far too many deadbeat dads.

What he would have given to have been the proud father sitting here beside his wife, offering her solace and hope in a time of such agonizing uncertainty. Instead he was but a working man's cowboy daunted by the prospect of catching this woman's tears.

"Mel, I..." he started to say.

Just then the door swung open, and the doctor stepped inside the room. He was a young man, barely in his thirties with a nervous demeanor that inspired little confidence. His gaze darted back and forth between the patient and the formidable man at her side.

He introduced himself as Jim Yangston and said he had been privileged to be one of Grace's many friends in the medical establishment. Pausing to draw a smile, he studied Melodie's grave expression and leapt to a conclusion that rocked the world beneath her feet.

"Knowing your mother as well as I did, would it be safe to assume you share her belief in prayer?"

Chapter Eleven

Melodie didn't answer right away. Having forsaken prayer when her life had seemed a bleak and endless desert, she wasn't sure it was honest to suddenly profess herself a believer. That old saying about there being no atheists in foxholes came to mind. In a time of such dire need, Melodie couldn't help wondering what belief in prayer could possibly hurt.

She looked at the nervous young man standing at the foot of her bed and tried to judge his intent. If he was trying to let her down gently, he was failing miserably. Good, bad or indifferent, Melodie was the type who preferred her news straight up.

"Why do you want to know?" she demanded, her voice sounding detached from her body.

The doctor responded first with an explanation of the results of the test that had been run. It seemed Melodie was in grave danger of having a miscarriage that could well threaten her life as well as that of her unborn baby. If she could make it through the third month, the doctor thought it was possible that she might actually be able to carry the baby to term. Or at least deliver a premature baby later that had a better chance of surviving and being healthy.

It was only after his very technical explanation of her condition that the doctor launched into what at one time in Melodie's life she might have considered a New Age application of positive thinking upon one's health. Long ago the distinction between prayer and wishful thinking had blurred for her. It was all Melodie could do to keep from screaming.

How long was she going to be punished for past mistakes? The Biblical reference to the sins of the parents being visited upon the heads of their children echoed in her mind. Melodie grew furious at the thought. Would a merciful and just God punish an innocent baby for her mother's failings?

Since it seemed she was unable to respond to

the doctor's inquiry about her belief in prayer, Buck answered in her place.

"I wholeheartedly believe in the power of prayer," he professed.

Though he was responding to the doctor, he was looking at Melodie as if he were seeing right into her heart. She felt a stab of jealousy at the genuineness of his convictions. If only she could share his faith!

"Don't worry," Buck told her. "I believe enough for the both of us."

Melodie believed him. Gazing at him from behind a sheen of unshed tears, she thought that if anyone could procure her a miracle, Buck could. What she herself lacked in faith, Melodie assured him she more than made up for in hope. If certified doctors were willing to grant prayer a place in modern medicine, who was she to disavow its healing power?

Reaching out for Buck's hand, Melodie asked him to help her pray. He willingly obliged, giving her an encouraging smile and an assurance that she had nothing to fear in opening her heart up to God. The fact that Melodie's hand tingled for hours afterward struck her as strange. Hesitant to attribute it as a sign from heaven, she reminded herself that

Buck's touch always had an extraordinary effect upon her.

Miracles began the very next morning. When people started arriving with books, magazines, homemade delicacies and loving kindness, Melodie wasn't quite sure how to react. Burned once before and thus leery of their motives, she was afraid of being harassed once again about her past transgressions. The doctor had sternly warned her to avoid all instances of stress, but as a prisoner in her hospital bed, there was little she could manage in the way of escape.

By noon, Melodie was convinced that the steady stream of visitors into her room was not there to cast blame or to satisfy some ghastly need for new gossip. Indeed her old neighbors and even the minister seemed genuinely concerned for her health. Surprised by their show of support, she couldn't help but wonder if their actions were motivated more from their desire to appease Buck than from their own guilt or a need to set things right.

"Don't worry," Mrs. Solans assured her with a smile that made the Mona Lisa's seem hackneyed. As sincere as her husband, the good Reverend's wife exuded an air of confidence that Melodie found comforting. "We've put you on a prayer chain."

This particular prayer chain started with the local congregation, encircled the little community of Dubois, and extended by means of phone and e-mail far beyond the borders of Wyoming. Though Melodie had her doubts, she nonetheless thanked the dear lady for her time and concern. She suspected that even the most hardened skeptic would be hesitant in dismissing the awesome power of thousands of voices raised in unison asking for divine healing on her behalf.

That Cora Linn did not put in a personal appearance at her bedside both saddened and relieved Melodie. It saddened her because it was painful to think she had lost the respect of an old family friend and that there was nothing she could ever do to regain it. On the other hand, she was relieved that the crotchety old lady had enough integrity to stay away when an apology on her part would have been hypocritical.

She was likewise grateful that Judy Roes stayed away. Just imagining the scene in which Buck's old fiancée asked her if he was the baby's father was enough to send Melodie's blood pressure skyrocketing. Regardless of the truth, she supposed such speculations would be forthcoming. In such a small community it would be foolhardy to imagine otherwise. Understanding that the last thing she needed right now was any undo tension placing added strain upon her baby, Melodie chose to deal with ugly rumors later rather than sooner. She just hoped Buck's newfound religious belief would help him see things in the same judicious manner.

A sense of obligation compelled Melodie to call Randall's parents and inform them of her pregnancy. She was as surprised by the elation in their reaction to the news that they were to become grandparents as she was by the fear in their voice when she relayed the danger her baby was facing. She did not doubt her mother-in-law's tears were genuine. However much they blamed her for the loss of their son, the fact that she was carrying his heir did much to bridge the chasm between them. As despicable as her in-laws had been to her personally, Melodie vowed not to deprive them of a relationship with their grandchild should they choose to pursue one. By the time she hung up the phone, Melodie could feel a sense of healing settling over her weary soul.

Forty some odd hours since her admission to the hospital, Dr. Yangston reappeared at her bedside with the welcome news that her condition had stabilized. ''The drugs appear to have stopped the immediate danger of a miscarriage. What that means is that you can go home—provided that you promise to stay in bed. Like I said before, I believe if you can make it past the third month, you've got a good chance of carrying this baby to term.''

Refusing to entertain any other possibility, Melodie thanked the young man who took such personal interest in his patients. The idea of being incapacitated at home was certainly preferable to being laid up in the hospital. Because Buck promised not to let her lift so much as a finger around the ranch, the doctor signed her release papers. For the first time in her life, Melodie meekly allowed herself to be pushed to the curb in a wheelchair and lifted into the passenger side of Buck's pickup.

The prospect of doing nothing for a prolonged period of time was more daunting to her than any task that Zeus set forth for Jason and his Argonauts. She was a woman who defined herself by what she could do. Just sitting was as foreign to Melodie as speaking in tongues. But since this baby meant more to her than life itself, she was willing to do whatever it took to ensure its healthy delivery into the world. If the doctor had insisted she stand on her head for the duration of her pregnancy, she would have complied without complaint.

Nonetheless, Melodie felt terribly guilty about putting Buck in the position of baby-sitting her all the while trying to run their ranch single-handledly.

"Don't worry," he assured her. "The church ladies are all planning on taking turns checking up on you and bringing food. They all seem to feel that any pregnant woman in their midst who escaped notice is just too skinny for her baby's good."

Melodie grinned. "Tell them not to be too hard on themselves. I didn't even realize I was pregnant."

The very thought of having the "church ladies" as Buck called them visiting her daily was quite frankly disconcerting to someone who had so neatly categorized these people as a bunch of hypocrites. If anything could change her mind about their intentions, Melodie supposed it would be a bedridden state and too much time on her hands. The only good thing that she could discern about being treated as an invalid was being carried from the vehicle to her bed in Buck's strong arms. As much as Melodie tried to tell herself that she resented it, the sensation of being held against this man's heart was as close to heaven as she ever personally expected to get. The smell of woodsy aftershave blended with a scent that was musky and heady and totally masculine.

Buck seemed to think, however, that her pregnancy had rendered Melodie as fragile as a glass. He couldn't have placed her more gently upon the bedcovers than had she been a newborn herself. He made a great deal of setting a little bell on her bed stand in case she needed him. The fact that it was the same bell Grace had used to summon him gave Melodie a chill. She shivered visibly, causing Buck to make much ado about the inadequate heating in the old house.

She couldn't resist teasing him.

"For such a big, strong guy, you sure are a fussbudget."

The look Buck gave her in reply said he would put up with none of her nonsense.

Not wanting to risk his ire, Melodie turned suddenly serious. "You really don't have to act as my nursemaid. Taking care of mother like you did surely earned you enough grace to enter the kingdom of heaven many times over. When you consider the way I've treated you over the years—"

Refusing to let her continue, Buck leaned over the bed and put a definitive finger to her lips. A delectable finger, Melodie thought, tasting the sweetness of his touch.

"I didn't take care of Grace in hopes of some eternal reward. I loved your mother, Mel."

"I know," she whispered, fighting back tears. "And even though I failed her miserably, I loved her, too."

Buck nodded his head. "I know you did," he said. "And so did she."

Melodie squeezed her eyes shut to keep him for seeing how much that affirmation meant to her. By the time she opened them again, Buck had gone, leaving her alone to ponder whether his present concern was motivated by the same unselfish reasons. After all she had done to ruin his life, was it possible that he could still love her? Or did he simply feel an obligation to Grace's only grandchild?

Even in the midst of Randall's darkest days of depression, Melodie hadn't realized how slowly time could crawl by. Work had been her constant companion, and as such she had directed her attention to a myriad of physically and mentally challenging tasks that had kept her otherwise occupied every day.

Within the first twenty-four hours of confinement, television lived up to its reputation as a vast wasteland. One day of constrained soap operas, talk shows that would have more appropriately been dubbed scream shows and a string of moldy, old sitcoms was enough to compel Melodie to fling the remote control across the room. Never having been handy with embroidery, knitting or other such ladylike pursuits, she was soon at wit's end trying to occupy her time.

Much to her own surprise, she found herself actually looking forward to the daily visits of old neighbors. In her time of need, they seemed willing to put aside earlier transgressions. Melodie couldn't help but wonder just how big a part Buck had played in their sudden change of heart.

What sustained her through days of boredom and fear was the miracle growing inside her. Still too small to make itself known with a kick or fist pressed against her ribs, the baby felt like her own sweet secret. Every morning Melodie awoke wondering if she had conjured up this pregnancy in her dreams. When no one was around, she had taken to talking to the unborn babe, giving him or her advance advice on how not to give up on the world before having a chance to experience it firsthand.

She wondered if the infant would cause her heartache similar to that which she inflicted upon her own mother. No matter. The most precious gift of motherhood was its own reward. Melodie knew that nothing her child ever did would displace its beating heart from right beneath hers.

Buck's compassion was more than Melodie could understand on a purely logical level. That he was willing to put aside personal feelings to protect the life of a child that was not even his own was astonishing in itself. In light of the fact that this was the baby of a man he despised it was almost saintly.

Buck was feeling far less holy than Melodie might have suspected in the days and weeks that followed. Certainly nothing in his religion had prepared him for such a peculiar twist of fate. How could any man of decent moral character resent an innocent baby? *A baby he desperately wished was his.* The question haunted Buck.

It had been difficult enough accepting Melodie's change of heart where he was concerned years ago. To have her return home as his partner added insult to an old but yet raw injury. That Melodie's homecoming had ultimately caused him to sever his relationship with Judy made him feel a fool a hundred times over. On top of everything else, this pregnancy shattered Buck's illusion that Melodie's marriage had been cold and loveless. Despite everything to which she had alluded regarding Randall's flawed character, Melodie had not denied him her body. The thought sickened him.

Not a man inclined to looking for solutions to his problems in the bottom of a glass of whiskey, Buck nonetheless decided a drink among friends at the corner bar was certainly warranted on one particularly dismal night following a day in which hard physical labor failed to chase his demons away. He no more wanted to confront Melodie about his conflicted feelings than he wanted to face them himself. Frustrated by his inability to rise above petty emotion, he succumbed to the hope that his bitterness would go down easier if followed by a beer chaser.

That Buck had never come home so late was certainly none of Melodie's business, but that didn't make his behavior any less worrisome. Stretched out on the couch she counted the minutes by the changing of one mindless television program to another. She wondered if this was what parenting was going to be like: never laying one's head down upon a pillow with the same assurance of untroubled sleep as before one's children's entrance into the world. Just imagining waiting up for an errant son or daughter was enough to give one pause over the more alarming aspects of parenthood. In comparison, giving birth looked easy.

Melodie hardly had to remind herself that she was not Buck's mother. He'd had no real mother other than the woman who had born him and relinquished him to a world overburdened with unwanted children. Luckily both Melodie and Buck had had the benefit of Grace's loving influence. Lately, Melodie had taken to talking to her mother as if she were right there in the room. This benevolent vision whispered words of encouragement and wisdom that alternately had Melodie laughing and crying.

"Oh, Mom," she whispered into the dark corners of that old house, "how do you expect me to do this without you?"

The dubious answer to that question came in the front door in the form of Buck. He reeked of barroom smoke and the lingering odor of alcohol. Suspecting that she was the reason for this man's condition, Melodie felt a stab of guilt for all the trouble she had caused him. She was also righteously irritated that he had left her to worry without so much as a word of his whereabouts. All her feelings were, however, superseded by an overwhelming sense of relief that he was home safe and sound.

"Are you all right?" she called out.

"Just peachy," came the laconic reply.

Melodie watched him make his way slowly across the kitchen floor to the coffeepot. From there he proceeded to the refrigerator where he opened the upper freezer section. Buck stood there a long time with his back to her, causing her at last to ask just what he was doing.

"Do we have any frozen peas?" he mumbled back cryptically.

Melodie wondered if he was loaded. She hoped not. Drinking had never improved Randall's mood, and she was in no condition to argue with a belligerent drunk at this time of night. She most certainly wasn't about to cook for one.

"No peas and no *q*'s either," she quipped, hoping to keep the mood light if at all possible.

Now that Buck was home, she could finally get some sleep without worrying about him. Yawning, she tossed back the afghan Grace had woven to match the couch. Though the trip from the living room to the bedroom was only a matter of a few steps, Melodie worried every time she stood up whether to go to the bathroom or simply change her location. She was not alone in her fears.

When she sat up, Buck was instantly at her side, offering to carry her to the bed.

"What happened?" Melodie demanded to know, her hand fluttering in a healing gesture to the left side of his face which was bruised and already turning a sickly shade of purple.

"Just a little disagreement over a horse," he assured her.

It had been, in fact, a word very close in pronunciation to *horse* applied to Melodie that had launched Buck over the bar at three brothers, the drunkest of whom made the mistake of teasing him about living with a woman of questionable repute. Buck considered his own black eye regrettable, but he had to admit that it had felt good unleashing all his pent-up frustrations upon such deserving scoundrels. An added benefit was that word traveled fast in this community. It wouldn't take long for everyone to hear secondhand accounts of what he had said to set the record straight.

Anyone who suspected that he was involved in taking advantage of a grieving widow who was pregnant with her deceased husband's child could make an appointment to see him personally.

Afraid to actually touch him, Melodie's fingers fluttered nervously near Buck's wounds. A trickle of blood had dried at the corner of his mouth. In addition to numerous abrasions, in the morning he was going to have a fat lip to go with his black eye. Melodie wondered if he would feel the need to sport dark glasses at church on Sunday. It was her understanding that the good minister looked poorly upon barroom brawls involving their more prominent parishioners.

"I hope you didn't earn this on my account," she said, brushing a stray lock of dark hair away from his eye and watching his response carefully to see if she had guessed right about the source of his difficulties.

Buck winced.

Melodie wasn't sure if it was from the truth or his injuries.

"Let me find something to take the swelling down," she offered.

Buck laid a restraining hand upon her shoulder as she strained to get up from the couch.

"I'm okay," he reassured her firmly. "How about you?"

Melodie forced a smile. How like him to be concerned about her when he was the one bleeding. She sincerely doubted whether he really wanted to hear about her day of watching the wallpaper fade or how, even being off her feet, her ankles were swelling, how she had never felt more helpless or unattractive in her life, or how being unable to focus her mind and body upon the physical demands of work, her thoughts kept turning down dark avenues where guilt and fear were her most faithful companions.

"I'm fine."

Buck was fooled neither by her smile nor her words.

"What a pair we are," he noted, shaking his head at the image they presented the world.

He grabbed a bottle of lotion on the floor beside her. Opening the lid, he discovered it smelled of papaya and kiwis. Buck poured a generous amount of the fruity, feminine potion into one hand. Shifting his position to the end of the couch, he pulled back the blankets tucked around her legs. He lathered the lotion in both hands and made her an offer no sane woman would refuse.

"Why don't you let me give you a foot rub?"

"You don't have to do that," she protested, kicking the covers free.

The manner in which Buck took her left foot carefully into his hand reminded Melodie of a picture from an old storybook from her childhood in which Prince Charming fit Cinderella's foot in a delicate glass slipper. Melodie shook her head to rid herself of the ridiculous image. She was far too old to be indulging in silly fantasies. For heaven's sake, who ever heard of a pregnant, incapacitated Cinderella?

Buck's hands were callused but infinitely gentle as he began to work his healing magic.

"This is definitely the sweetest thing anyone has ever done for me."

In the entire course of her marriage, Randall had never touched her so tenderly.

This was the way Melodie had always dreamed marriage could be at its finest: the gentle ministering of each other's pains and heartaches, the steadfast support of each other's dreams and the simple delight of each other's company.

The next thing she knew, Buck was tucking her blankets back around her feet. When he reached for the brush on the end table next to the couch, Melodie was glad for an excuse to extend their time together. Despite the lateness of the hour and the ragged condition of their bodies, it seemed neither one of them was ready to call it a night.

Complaining that she was going to develop bedsores if she didn't get up and move around a little, she had managed a short shower earlier in the day, taking care not to slip and fall. Never again would she take such simple tasks as bathing and washing her hair for granted again. Melodie had attempted to brush her hair after it dried, but rubbing it against a pillow for the better part of the day had left it a mess of snarls. She couldn't help but wonder if Buck wasn't offering his services simply because he found her a frightful sight. Pregnant, devoid of makeup and wearing a pair of baggy flannel pajamas, Melodie imagined herself the least sexy woman on the entire planet.

Had Buck been able to read her mind, he certainly would have disagreed. Her silken tresses shone in the dimly lighted room like moonlight spilling into his hands. Such was the stuff with which fair Rapunzel had lured her handsome prince. Guessing that Melodie's scalp was far more sensitive than the maiden who had let her suitor use her mane as a rope to climb, Buck was far gentler as he ran the brush through her hair. He couldn't remember touching anything so fine or beautiful. He was glad that this woman hadn't the time to succumb to contemporary fashion advice and cut her lovely locks into a chic, shorter style.

Little was said in words as Buck continued brushing Melodie's hair until it magically came alight with static electricity and crackled in his hands. Much was said in the silence of two separate hearts learning to beat again as one while forgiveness seeped into that little old house like the warmth emanating from a glowing potbellied stove.

Chapter Twelve

Buck did not wear dark glasses to church the following Sunday in an attempt to hide his disreputable shiner from the congregation, proving to Melodie once and for all that he really didn't care what other people thought of him. She smiled to think that beneath his more mature, devout veneer, there was still a bit of the rebel. If anyone was brave or foolish enough to question him about his black eye, Buck did not relay that information when he returned home later that day.

From her alternating vantage points between the bed and the couch, Melodie watched the days lengthening outside the window. Snow became a forgotten memory as brightly colored tulips pushed their way through recently frozen soil. The cheerful buds that Buck cut and placed in a vase on the end table in the living room reminded Melodie of the woman who planted them. She was grateful that such reminiscences no longer caused her heart to shrink inside her chest as they had when she first arrived home. Indeed, memories of Grace were becoming less painful and more temperate with the warming temperature.

"Mom would have loved them," Melodie heard herself saying. Placing her hand across her growing tummy, she whispered to the baby growing inside her. "She surely would have loved you, too." Casting a glance at the flowers beside her, she amended the comment so that it was in present tense. "She does love you, sweetheart."

To be sure, Melodie felt her mother's presence so often and in so many ways that it was difficult for her to imagine Grace as being truly gone. She was still in the habit of making frequent appearances in her daughter's dreams. Also she seemed determined to make herself known in the multitude of uncommon reminders that kept popping up in sights, sounds and smells all around the house. Despite her hard-fought indifference to belief in an afterlife, Melodie couldn't help but consider the possibility that her mother was truly someplace nearby, healthy and happy and watching over her infant grandchild.

Thoughts of heavenly guidance from beyond were not new to Melodie, but like her faith in God, they had simply been misplaced for a very long time. Some stubborn thing inside her refused to believe that something as precious and fine as Grace's life had ended with her last breath. Perhaps it was the multitude of prayers storming the gates of heaven on her behalf that changed her mind and her outlook in the end. Perhaps it was being the recipient of her neighbors' daily acts of kindness.

More than likely it was simply being near Buck's innate goodness.

Feeling the baby inside her growing stronger every day, Melodie's heart rejoiced as hope took up permanent residence in the home she was privileged to share with such a good and honorable man. When the banner day marking the beginning of Melodie's second trimester arrived at last, Buck carefully loaded her up into the vehicle for a trip to the doctor's office. He assured her that taking time out of his busy schedule was no inconvenience at all. Once again, Melodie felt the thrill of being carried in a pair of arms strong enough to carry the weight of the entire world without complaint, without bending a spine straightened by hardship and faith.

Having allowed Buck the dubious privilege of rubbing her feet, combing her hair and generally waiting on her like a paid servant for the last few weeks, Melodie hoped he wouldn't mind that she nestled her head against his shoulder and drank in his wonderful, masculine scent. Wrapping her arms around his neck, she held on longer than necessary, regretting the moment when he placed her safely in the passenger seat and took away her excuse to snuggle tight.

During the drive, Buck resorted to teasing in an attempt to lighten the mood. He noted the need to extend the seat belt beyond its previous setting from the last time she made a similar trip home from the hospital. Though Melodie made a disparaging remark about her weight in contrast to that of a beached whale, she knew it was a good sign for her baby and refused to let vanity rule her head in regard to her healthy eating habits.

Doctor Yangston confirmed Melodie's own prognosis with a smile broad enough to slap on a Halloween pumpkin. She could see why her mother had taken such a liking to the doctor who first confirmed her pregnancy.

''It appears that the medication you're on has

done the trick, and the imminent danger of a miscarriage has passed. Don't get me wrong," he told her, holding up his hands in a warning gesture. "I don't want you running any foot races, but I think it's safe enough for you to actually get up and walk around a little every now and then. That is, as long as someone is around, just in case something should happen."

It was all Melodie could do to keep from shouting in jubilation. During her confinement, she'd had plenty of time to catch up on her reading, and she knew the third month of one's pregnancy was generally considered the most precarious. Placing a grateful peck on the doctor's cheek, she claimed a moral victory in making it to month four and assured the good doctor that she would do nothing to risk her baby's health.

Though the sonogram promised to be the highlight of the visit, when Doctor Yangston announced it, Buck promptly got up to leave.

"I'll just wait for you in the reception room," he said with all-endearing male distress at the prospect of some unpleasant, complicated procedure being performed in his presence.

"Wouldn't you like to stay?" Melodie asked him.

The accompanying look in those pretty blue

eyes assured Buck that he was not being asked out of some misplaced sense of courtesy but rather because Melodie really wanted him there. Much to his own surprise, he discovered that he, too, very much wanted to be present for this momentous occasion. Although he had no part in this baby's conception, he felt tied to this fatherless infant by something more binding than blood. With no further need of encouragement, he gave Melodie a smile and sat back down.

The gel the doctor smeared on Melodie's tiny belly bulge was cold and made her flinch. Mistaking the reaction for pain, Buck reached for her hand. Not bothering to explain away the misperception, Melodie held on tight, sensing that this man's touch was an umbilical cord to the universe itself. That a man's touch could be so gentle and reassuring at the same time was as great a mystery to her as was the image that appeared on the doctor's tiny screen.

Though Melodie couldn't make out anything but gray cloudy skies, Buck leaned forward in awe. He seemed perfectly capable of following the doctor's descriptions and ultimately satisfied with his professional opinion that everything looked perfectly normal. Melodie's sigh of relief at their mutual prognostication emanated from somewhere deep within her very soul. Valiantly, she held her tears at bay—right up until the doctor put his stethoscope on her tummy. When the *whoosh, whoosh, whoosh* sound of the baby's healthy heart filled the room with its amplified sound, Melodie was certain that she had never in her life heard sweeter music.

Buck passed her a tissue and turned slightly away so that she could not see the moisture in his own eyes. "I told you everything was going to be just fine," he mumbled.

Anyone peeking into the examining room would have thought they had stumbled upon a husband and wife sharing a very special moment. Melodie herself had a hard time remembering at times that they were not married. But as much as she wished otherwise, Buck was not this child's father. She most assuredly didn't want him to feel pressured by Doctor Yangston's inquiries about who was going to act as her coach at the birthing. Had Grace been alive, Melodie would have asked her mother to be at her side. As it was, the doctor's innocent question merely underscored just how truly alone she was in the world.

"I've assisted at enough animal birthings that I think I'll be able to manage just fine by myself," she said in what she hoped came off as a light, self-assured tone. After all, what good would it do anyone to admit how utterly terrified she was?

"I'd like to be there for you." Buck's voice was strong and uncompromising as he squeezed her hand and made her entire body tingle. "For you and the baby," he added. "That is, if you want me."

Melodie felt her chest tighten as her heart expanded with gratitude. That Buck had offered meant more to her than she could ever put into words. To be quite frank about it, she simply couldn't imagine placing herself in such a compromising position as giving birth with this man in the same room.

Nor could she imagine undertaking such a sacred, frightening event without him.

"Are you sure that you won't pass out on me?" she queried, squinting at him with skeptical blue eyes.

Buck guffawed at the very thought. Having spent much of his life learning the fine art of animal husbandry, he felt certain that he could lend the doctor a hand if need be himself. That he'd never been present at the birth of a human life didn't daunt him one bit. He certainly didn't figure Melodie for a screamer. In fact, he was so sure of her fortitude that he didn't even bother asking her if she intended to endure the accompanying pain in the typically stoic manner that he'd come to expect from her. He assumed that out of concern for her baby she would likely forswear any drugs to dull the discomfort.

The doctor shook his head at this protective cowboy's cockiness. "The bigger they are, the harder they fall," he said philosophically slapping Buck on the back and winking at Melodie over his shoulder.

They left the clinic a half an hour later in high spirits. The day was warm and the sun inviting as Melodie walked to the vehicle on her own two feet. It was an achievement she did not take lightly. She desperately wanted to believe that the worst was over. The nausea that had her reaching for crackers the first thing every morning was at last beginning to abate, and the overwhelming sense of exhaustion that characterized her first trimester was waning as well. The doctor's assurance that her baby was indeed healthy inside the safety of her womb had Melodie walking on air. If she had known the words to any apt show tune, she just might have burst into song as Buck opened the door for her and helped her in.

Her feeling of euphoria was as infectious as her smile.

"Are you hungry?" Buck asked, knowing the answer already. Lately she had developed an appetite that could put NFL linebackers to shame. Eating for two certainly agreed with her.

"Ravenous," she acknowledged, rubbing her tummy.

Buck pulled into the local grocery store's parking lot, promising to be back in a jiff. Ten minutes later, he returned carrying a sack bulging with goodies. The smell of fried chicken, crispy fries and apple pie filled the cab of the pickup and made Melodie's stomach growl in eagerness. It was all Buck could do to keep her from diving in on the spot.

"If you can wait a little longer, there's someplace special I'd like to take you," he said. "That is, if you feel up for a picnic."

Having been cooped up for so long, Melodie was delighted at the prospect. She was afraid that her naturally pale complexion was taking on a sallow tone. Nothing could have sounded more heavenly to her on a day such as today than an old-fashioned picnic with the man she had loved since childhood. It was her fondest wish that Buck would be a part of her baby's life. In today's difficult world, she knew every little boy and girl needed positive male role models.

Especially those without fathers of their own to guide them.

She was surprised when Buck passed City Park and drove in the direction of the ranch. When he pulled off the main highway and onto a little-known service road, she had a good idea where he was taking her. Soon enough the river came into view, and Melodie recognized the site of her favorite childhood haunt as her old tree house loomed on the horizon.

With its garland of early flowers, June brought hope to a landscape weary of the cold's stern and tenacious grasp. The last time they had come here together and Buck had pushed her on that old rope swing, there had been snow on the ground. That simple childish act had caused such a rush of memories to come flooding back when Melodie revisited the site that she'd fled from the place as if actually trying to outrun the ghosts of her past. Today she felt no such qualms.

The thought of consecrating their old stomping grounds with forgiveness and friendship was the perfect way to herald the coming of summer. Though the tree house was just a short jaunt from where Buck parked the vehicle, he was not about to let Melodie risk walking the distance herself. The ground was too uneven, he said. Though Melodie reminded him of the doctor's permission to exercise lightly, she ultimately succumbed to the indulgence of being carried in his arms one more time. She saw no reason not to take advantage of her condition for as long as she could.

Not wanting him to make two trips, Melodie insisted on carrying the sack of groceries herself. Luckily not even the scrumptious aroma of fried chicken could overpower the subtle scent of Buck's aftershave tickling her senses. It blended with the smell of pure mountain air and the fragrance of sage carried on a breeze that stirred the grass. Always ready for car trouble during the cold winter months, Buck brought a blanket from behind the seat of his vehicle. He proceeded to spread it out on the ground beneath the boughs of a cottonwood they both had come to think of as a personal friend in their childhood.

The scars of their initials were still visible in the trunk of that beloved old tree. Running a finger over the ridges in the gnarly bark, Melodie wondered aloud about the box of treasures she had left inside hidden away in a secret spot within that tree house for posterity. Though unable to remember exactly what she had left behind when she had embarked upon that fateful journey to college, she feared that the contents might well be incriminating.

The last thing she wanted was to push Buck away from her today of all days. The bubble of coexistence that they had worked out was far too fragile to be poked at by any pins from the past. However imperfect their living arrangements, Melodie did not want to think about the day Buck would have to leave. With childish determination to ignore that which she could, she decided to postpone such dreary thoughts until the baby was here. Then she could share the emptiness inside her with someone innocent and totally nonjudgmental.

Buck wasn't one to break his word. Having promised to be there for Melodie throughout her pregnancy, she knew he would be. She smiled enigmatically and passed him a piece of chicken. Although the lemonade was just from a can, it was sweet and nonetheless tasted of summer. Plastic forks dug into a shared container of potato salad, and Melodie good-naturedly wiped Buck's chin with a napkin.

Thanking her, he held her tenderly in a gaze that suspended time and made Melodie's heart miss several beats. All lingering signs of resentment were gone from those cougar gold eyes. Still Melodie was hesitant to read anything more into that

look than friendship. Knowing how vulnerable she
was to him, Melodie lowered her eyes to the
ground. The Arapaho design of that old woven
blanket blurred into indiscriminate spinning pat-
terns before she allowed herself to look up again.

Insisting that she was not to climb up the rickety
steps into the tree house to retrieve any supposed
treasures, Buck volunteered to go himself. Melodie
said it would be all right only if he promised to
return the container to her unopened. Stretching
her body across the length of the blanket she
watched him maneuver the boards she and Grace
had nailed into the tree trunk so many years ago.
Melodie gasped when one of the old boards came
loose altogether beneath Buck's weight. Thinking
fast, he grabbed hold of a low branch. Pulling himself up with a grunt, he disappeared inside a tree
house that had once upon a time seemed cavern-
ous.

Melodie giggled to hear his comments upon hit-
ting his head on the low ceiling. She doubted
whether anything physical remained of her memories. She liked to think that some other boy and
girl had stumbled upon this hallowed spot and
made it their own.

"I found it!" Buck called out, not bothering to
mask the elation in his voice.

Melodie's heart leapt like a wild horse bucking in fear at the prospect of being corralled. "Don't you dare sneak a peak," she hollered to him.

Tucking the box beneath one arm, Buck proceeded to climb down from his perch.

"You look like some great big bird ready to take flight," Melodie commented.

She wasn't about to tell him that with the sun in her eyes he really looked more like an angel arriving special delivery. A mouthwatering, masculine, warrior angel straight out of her dreams. The sight was enough to make her sigh as Buck emerged from the boughs of that sturdy, old tree and dropped to the ground beside her.

"Something wrong?" he asked.

"No, something very right," she replied with a satisfied smile that reflected all that was right with the world.

Despite everything that she had been through, the truth was Melodie had never been happier. Staring up into the lacework of branches and blue sky overhead, she felt as if heaven were truly watching over her. She savored each day that brought her baby closer to birth and relished the thought of getting big enough to don official pregnancy clothes. The thought of an innocent infant nestled and nurtured beneath her heart was truly miraculous, all the more so because she had long ago given up on her dream of ever conceiving a child.

Though her joy was offset by the tragic loss of her mother, Melodie was at last coming to terms with the concept that Grace had moved on to a happier plane, a place where there was no more pain and struggle. The thought brought her comfort, as did the growing realization that her mother had not taken any resentment with her from this world. Melodie knew that the overwhelming guilt she felt would probably never completely go away. Lately, however, it was lightened by a sense of gratitude for the woman who had deliberately gotten Buck and her daughter back together again.

Perhaps it wasn't in the romantic way that Melodie secretly dreamed, but it brought her great joy nonetheless. After spending time in a twisted relationship with someone who thought controlling a person was the same as loving another, it was enough for her to simply maintain a friendship with a man who meant so much to her. Enough that she would willingly put away her love for him just so that she could continue being near him.

Fearing one glance at her face would let him read her conflicting emotions, she kept her eyes trained on his cowboy boots. It was a temporary ploy at best as Buck settled down beside her on the blanket and invaded her space, her heart and her soul. He placed the small wooden box between them.

The cedar box was not in good shape because of rain and snow that had worked their way through the rough lumber of the tree house roof. Still, the mere sight of it carried Melodie back in time. Back to when her mother had bought her the souvenir to remember a trip to the Black Hills when she was only ten years old.

Even if it meant opening that Pandora's box in Buck's presence, Melodie felt a sudden urgency to reclaim her childish treasures. Picking it up reverently, she hoped Buck didn't notice how her hands trembled when she opened the rusty latch. Despite its stained cover, the contents of the box had indeed withstood the test of time. Much to her own surprise, Melodie's personal time capsule remained intact. A collection of original poetry from high school, a charm bracelet from elementary school, her favorite novel of all times, a lucky penny and a yellowed strip of photographs of Buck and her snapped in one of those silly mall booths was all that Melodie left behind when she had embarked upon that fateful journey to college.

That and her heart of course.

Who would have thought she would have ever become such an emotional creature, stirred by the scent of cedar and lost dreams? As much as Melodie would have liked to blame the tears that sprang to her eyes upon the raging hormones of pregnancy, she refused to lie to herself. Would that her bitter regrets regarding her past with Buck turn to sweeter memories like those she was coming to cherish about her mother....

Taking the strip of brittle old photographs from Melodie, Buck placed them gently in the palm of his hand. The smiling faces of their youth caught forever on film asked the question that no one dared to answer.

How could they have been so blindly naive about protecting their once-in-a-lifetime love?

Trying to direct the conversation along a less painful avenue, Melodie pointed at a neatly folded piece of paper peering out of his shirt pocket. She hadn't noticed it there before his foray into the tree house.

"What's this?" she asked, grabbing for it.

Buck pulled away before she could get her hands on it.

"Nothing," he assured her.

Melodie studied his expression. He knew a whole lot more than he was letting on.

"Nothing?"

Little did Melodie know that many years ago, Buck had added his own "treasure" to her hiding place. Folded neatly against his heart lay the hand-drawn plans of the very house he had once planned on building for her when they were married. The original plans were yellowed with age. Long ago he'd had official blueprints drawn up from these humble designs. Many times he had been tempted to pitch those plans that were still tucked away in the back of his desk drawer. Having paid good money for them at a time when he had so precious little, he told himself that it was the cost alone that kept him from tossing them.

Truth was they had cost him more dearly than he liked to admit. He suspected that it was a sin to part with one's dreams prematurely, no matter how futile they might seem.

That he had never seriously thought about using the same plans to build a house for Judy had been only one indication that he had no business considering a future with her. These plans were a sacred part of his past. The best part of his life, if he could allow himself to admit it. He could not imagine sharing them with anyone but Melodie.

Living with her under the same roof had inevitably brought it all back: the warmth of her smile, the gentleness of her touch, the strong curve of her jaw when she set it against the world, the simple pleasure of sharing her company and the attraction that even time could not extinguish.

In the end, Buck simply handed over the plans to Melodie, a gift from their past that he hoped would mean as much to her as it did to him. Certainly she was in too fragile a condition to be wrestling him like they had when they were kids, and Buck saw no point in hiding his true feelings from her any longer.

As his soul mate, she had a right to know and share in his pain.

Melodie unfolded the plans as carefully as if she were opening a pirate's treasure map, which indeed she was. It took her no longer to discern that it was Buck's writing than that what she held in her hands were the plans to a house.

"Why, these are yours," she said, wrinkling her brow in confusion. "What are they doing here?"

"Look closely at them," Buck told her, fighting the old surge of pride that he had felt when he'd first penned them.

The log and natural stone facade, many windows, open-beamed ceilings, fireplace and loft bedroom were exactly as if Melodie had planned the layout herself. It appeared that Buck had not only listened to her schoolgirl ramblings about the house she hoped to someday share with him but had also taken the first step to making those dreams a reality. Proof of his endeavor to make her a perfect life lay unfurled in her lap. As a breeze tugged at its fragile edges, Melodie saw an image of her dreams dancing in the sky like a wild kite free of any earthbound strings.

"Oh, Buck," she murmured, overcome with regret for what she had lost.

Far more than a house, it was a home. It was a heart beating right there in her hands.

"Can you ever forgive me for being so stupid?" she asked in a whisper.

"Only if you can forgive me in turn," he rejoined, his voice soft and gentle. Putting his hands on either side of her head, he turned Melodie so that she was looking directly across the river.

"I want you to look over there," he said pointing her gaze to a grassy knoll. "That's where I was going to build you the castle of your dreams. The reason I put in so many windows is that I remember you saying how much you'd like watching the seasons change on the river."

On and on he went, describing in loving detail all the special features he'd included on her behalf. After all these years, the vision was as clear in his mind as the day he'd penciled it all in. Unable to keep the tears from welling up inside her, Melodie allowed them to fall freely down her face as she openly wept for all that she had lost.

"Look hard," he told her. "Can you see it?"

Though tears blurred Melodie's vision, she could indeed see it as vividly as if the logs had been notched and nails actually driven. In addition to the structure itself, beautiful in its simple, clean lines, she could make out several children playing joyfully in the front yard. Her throat tightened around the images of what might have been.

What should have been!

"Please don't ask me to do this," she implored. It just hurt too much to pretend that it didn't.

"Admittedly, I was a little premature when I drew these plans up," Buck told her with a sad little laugh of chagrin. "I forgot to plan for children. Luckily, there's still time to modify the design to include a nursery for the baby. Maybe even add a few more bedrooms if you think you'd like to have children with me someday."

Turning her face away from the scene he had just described, Buck compelled her to look directly at him. Melodie gaped at him as if he were mad. He couldn't possibly mean what she thought he had said. That his eyes were open wide and as vulnerable to her rebuff as he had been as a boy made her question her own sanity.

Her voice quavered like an aspen leaf in the wind as she asked, "What are you saying?"

"What I'm saying," Buck repeated, removing his hands from her and shifting his position so that he was kneeling before her, "or rather what I'm asking, is will you marry me?"

His voice sounded very far away to Melodie. Perhaps she had fallen asleep upon this blanket on this lovely day and she was dreaming the perfect dream. If so, she never wanted to be awakened. Her skin tingled where his hands had lingered upon her cheeks, where the pads of his thumbs were acting as windshield wipers to dry her tears. Reaching out to touch him, Melodie wanted to make sure she wasn't hallucinating.

"Let's put the past behind us, Mel, and focus on the rest of our lives. A future filled with laughter and children. You do want more children, don't you?"

That Buck's voice grew stronger intensified the feeling that this conversation was not some figment of Melodie's imagination. A dream come true, her conscience was nonetheless jarred by the mention of children. What if he was offering to marry her for all the wrong reasons? Out of some misguided sense of obligation to Grace's grandchild? Or worse yet, out of pity for a single mother unable to make it on her own?

"You don't have to marry me simply because of the baby I'm carrying. A baby," she reminded him gently, "that you didn't father. Having married for the wrong reasons once before, I don't want you sacrificing your happiness for mine. I'm not anybody's spiritual charity case, Buck Foster. I certainly don't want you thinking of me as your proverbial ticket into heaven."

The proud expression she wore made Buck smile. How had he managed to fall in love with such a headstrong woman not once but twice in the same lifetime?

"Let me assure you, sweetheart, that my proposal is based entirely on my feelings for you, not for your baby, and certainly not to elevate my standing in the eyes of God or anyone else in this community. Although," he added thoughtfully, "I do have to admit that nothing could make me happier than providing you and this baby with the kind of stability and unconditional love that I never had as a child."

His thoughts drifted back to a time in his life when the sting of rejection was with him constantly. Placing a protective hand upon Melodie's tummy, he told her, "I promise to love this child as my own. As I love you, Little Bit, and always have. As Grace loved me without regard to who sired me. With my whole heart and body and soul. In the past, now and forever, I love you."

Hearing this rugged cowboy speak the words of deeply felt poetry, Melodie wondered whether a heart could truly overflow with happiness. She had heard the expression, but never before had she truly experienced it. Indeed, a heart once battered and hidden from the rest of the world by a wall she'd built herself, rock by bloody rock, threatened to explode in her chest. Deep, untidy passions charted her course for the future. Her universe, so recently devoid of love, faith and hope was suddenly spilling over with a spiritual abundance she could never have imagined before.

So there could be no mistaking her motivation, Melodie leaned forward and kissed Buck. Soundly. If ever she believed that God was punishing her for past mistakes, those misgivings melted away beneath a sun too bright to allow shadows into even the darkest corners of her mind.

"Yes!" she told him, not bothering to unwrap her arms from around his neck. "Yes, I will marry you, Buck Foster, whenever you want, wherever you want. And I promise to make you a good wife and to have as many children as you have rooms in your heart and house for.''

"Before the baby is born, if that's all right with you,'' he said, his voice gruff with emotion, proving once again that he didn't care at all about what anyone else thought. If she wanted a white pregnancy wedding dress, he couldn't have cared less. The sooner they were married the better as far as Buck was concerned. Having lost this woman once in his life, he wasn't about to risk losing her again.

Beneath the boughs of a cottonwood bursting with the natural rebirth of spring, they kissed. And in between sweet, tender kisses, they made plans for a wedding—and, more important, for the marriage that was to follow.

Deciding that Grace's home was too cluttered with sad memories, they studied the plans that Buck had drawn up those many years ago and adapted them to suit their present needs. Melodie most certainly did want brothers and sisters for the baby who was going to arrive in a few short months. Studying the banks of the scenic Wind River, they added more bedrooms and storage and windows to their plans and filled their dream home with faith, hope, love and a lifetime of wonderful memories.

Epilogue

Melodie deliberately ignored the pained sigh from the minister standing at the pulpit as she turned to fuss over the baby in her lap. Seven years ago when Reverend Solans had married Buck and her in this very church welcoming them as a couple into the congregation, she doubted whether he had so much as an inkling that he would someday be transferred to a foreign mission thereby leaving his youthful replacement so unprepared for the burgeoning family sitting in the third row from the front. Sitting was, of course, a charitable term for the performance that her rambunctious children provided free of charge during services every week.

Buck was fond of saying that Gracie was the spitting image of her. Melodie didn't bother disputing the claim. Her daughter's vivid blue eyes snapped in annoyance at the self-appointed task of wrangling her little brothers into a semi-still state of religious observance. Identical bookends of their father, the twins had fidgeting down to an actual art form. Gracie took after Melodie in more than just her fair looks. The little girl was particularly stubborn, and when she stuck out her chin, there was no question that she meant business. Her mother anticipated that retribution would begin directly after services.

In her properly ironed Sunday best, Gracie appeared to be such a good little mother at the tender age of seven that her parents worried she might spend the rest of her life attempting to rescue and refine her younger siblings. If left to her own devices, they feared it wouldn't be many years before Gracie was playing matchmaker for the twins and trying to foist them upon some poor unsuspecting females who didn't know better than to look past the boys' good looks. Already, grown women were commenting on their matched set of amber eyes and long eyelashes. Melodie could only hope that heaven would rush to help the poor girls who fell for her dynamic duo!

Covertly, Joey kicked Justin beneath the pew, causing him to let out a yelp of pain. Melodie gave them both a warning glance. With yet another baby resting under her chin, she refused to let her children's antics distract her from this special time allocated for God. She shared a sympathetic look with Buck as he proceeded to take matters into his own hands. Little had she known when she returned home to the Rocky Mountains that she would find happiness with the good man sitting beside her, his chest puffed out in pride.

Melodie doubted whether the earnest minister would dare reproach her about the effect her children's behavior was having upon his sermon if only because she didn't think he was brave or foolish enough to broach the subject in front of Buck. Definitely the proudest father in the whole community, he lavished attention upon each and every member of his family. Determined they would never know the rejection he felt as a child at the hands of his own flesh and blood, he did everything in his power to make sure that they understood his love was unconditional. He knew first hand how much more children have need of role models than of critics.

Not that Buck intended coddling their children and rendering them unfit for the real world. His plans for their future included hard work, weekly attendance at church, attention to schooling and, above all, respect for their mother. He appreciated the fact that the most important thing a man can do for his children is to love their mother the way he did. The good Lord as well as every member of the congregation was fully aware of just how deeply he loved his wife.

Lifting Joey up and placing him securely in his lap so that he could no longer pester his brother with impunity, Buck handed Justin a picture book in hopes of capturing his attention for at least a few minutes. Then he reached for his wife's hand. Melodie turned that rapt expression from the altar to gaze upon her husband's face. Seeing the love reflected in his eyes made her sigh with perfect contentment. Everything important in this world was gathered about her, and she was made whole in the midst of their love.

Not caring a whit for whether it broached the conventions of church decorum, she rested her head for a moment upon Buck's strong shoulder. Automatically his arm went around her, drawing her nearer to his heart. Having spent so much of their youth giving people something to talk about, they saw no reason to change their ways at this stage in their lives. Buck placed a kiss upon the top of his wife's golden head and whispered something in her ear. Something that caused her to blush and made the group of teenagers sitting behind them giggle in speculation.

Squeezing Buck's hand, Melodie assured him that nothing could ever sever the connection between them. Like the hands intertwined over the top of the sleeping baby cradled in her arms, their souls were truly joined together forever. Knowing that there was no end to a love that was learned over and over again every day, Melodie smiled as she looked up at the minister and nodded for him to continue.

*   *   *   *   *

Dear Reader,

This book has truly been a labor of love for me. Numerous hurdles had to be overcome before it ever reached your hands. Know that I am honored that it has found a home with you. The theme of redemption explored in these pages gives meaning to my own life, and I dearly hope to yours, as well. May your sojourn with the characters who are such a part of my heart touch you as deeply as they have me. God bless you and keep you ever close to your dreams.

With sincere appreciation,

Cathleen Connors

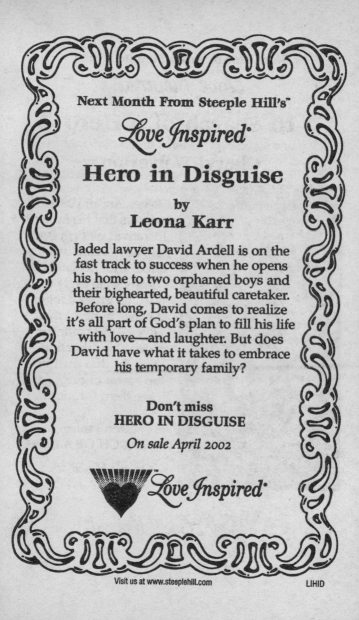

Next Month From
Steeple Hill's™

Love Inspired®

Something Beautiful

by
Lenora Worth

Daredevil Lucas Dorsette relishes flirting
with danger. However, the reckless pilot
discovers a new appreciation for life
when he falls in love with a stunning
supermodel who shows him the true
meaning of courage. But will their faith
help them face an uncertain future?

**Don't miss
SOMETHING BEAUTIFUL**

On sale April 2002

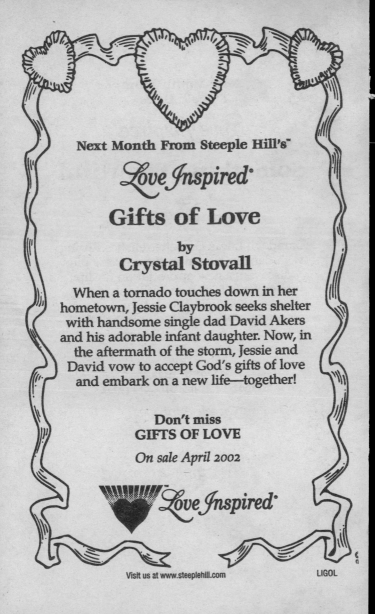

Next Month From Steeple Hill's™

Love Inspired®

Gifts of Love

by
Crystal Stovall

When a tornado touches down in her
hometown, Jessie Claybrook seeks shelter
with handsome single dad David Akers
and his adorable infant daughter. Now, in
the aftermath of the storm, Jessie and
David vow to accept God's gifts of love
and embark on a new life—together!

**Don't miss
GIFTS OF LOVE**

On sale April 2002

Love Inspired®